RESTLESS ROCKSTAR

THE BURNT CLOVERS

GINA AZZI

ONE

DEREK

APRIL 13

11:47 *a.m.*

Stellina,

God, I miss you. I understand why you won't take my calls, but I wish I could hear your voice. Communicating like this is tough, but that's because I'm a selfish bastard who wants unfettered access to you all the damn time.

I'm sorry, again, for leaving the way I did. It was—fuck, a head trip. I can't believe I came face-to-face with my father that way. I can't believe he fucking knows you. And, as much as you sing his praises, I hate that he knows you in a way, on a level, that I don't.

My head is a mess. My feelings all over the damn place. I'm angry and confused and exhausted. But mostly, I'm lonely. I fucking miss you, little star. Even though I don't deserve you in my life, I'm grateful you haven't cut me out. At least, not entirely.

Let me know how you're doing.

Love,

Derek

. . .

APRIL 15

9:42 p.m.

Hey, Derek,

It's good to hear from you. I understand why you left. I get that unexpectedly meeting your dad is a lot to process. I just wish you could've processed it with me by your side. Still, I want to help you navigate this. I want to be a person in your life, even if I can't be there in a full capacity.

To be honest, it's too hard. The sound of your voice, knowing what we were planning for just a few months ago... I can't keep putting myself in that position. Right now, I think it's best that we proceed as friends. Please don't keep calling and leaving voice messages. When I'm ready to talk, I'll call you.

Take care of yourself,

Allegra

APRIL 21

11:52 p.m.

Stellina,

Fuck, this song is haunting me. Fitting, isn't it? The presence of you—whether in reality, or my mind, or my songs—has haunted me since day one. That's not a bad thing; it's probably the only thing in my life that matters besides the music.

You.

I'm so fucking sorry, beautiful girl, that I can't be the man you deserve. That I can't earn your trust and keep it. That I can't guard your heart without fucking shattering it.

Even though you will never be just my friend, I'll take

you any way I can get you. You're like a damn high in the best form possible. Like fucking sunshine. Your name shows up in my inbox and everything is better than it was a second earlier. So, let's keep emailing. And I'll stop with my voicemails. For now.

Most of my time is spent songwriting. Or fucking off in the studio. It's not the same though. Mav left for Costa Rica. He needs a break from dealing with Levi's, Jameson's, and my bullshit for as long as he has. Jameson is off-again with Amelia, nursing his bruised heart in a cabin by a lake in the middle of fucking nowhere. I'm sure they'll reconcile; they always do.

It does make me think about the toxicity of some relationships though. And fuck, little star, I hope that's not us. I don't want to be your downfall when you've always been my salvation.

Does that make me sound pussy-whipped like Jameson? I don't care if it does.

I've spoken some with your brother, as I'm sure he's told you. You don't have to move from the apartment. I don't want his money. I want you safe. And comfortable. And fucking happy.

Other than time with my music, I've started therapy. Dre hooked me up with a guy he knows, and while I'm not expecting miracles, I've gone to two sessions. The fact that I made an appointment for the third is a favorable sign. Dre sends his love and asks about you often.

Are you still working at Beirut?

Miss you,

Derek

APRIL 26

6:43 a.m.

Hi, Derek,

Sorry for taking so long to respond. I've been exhausted. Totally drained and not sleeping well, which explains the early morning email.

I'm proud of you for trying therapy. I'm glad you found a therapist who makes you want to schedule the next appointment. Miracles can happen—sometimes slowly—if you keep showing up and putting in the work. So, keep doing the work. You're capable of more than you think.

Thanks for the offer on the apartment, but now that Levi is bunking with me, a two-bedroom is a better option for us. Your security deposit and rent checks for the remainder of the year will be returned in the next week or two. Levi is handling it.

Since Levi moved in, I've been able to scale back. I'm no longer working at Beirut. Just taking classes and spending more time at the NGO. And more time with my friends and Levi. It's great to get to know my brother again. Better late than never, right?

We weren't toxic, Derek. Our timing just never lined up, not the way it should have. And that's okay.

Better something than nothing, right?

Stick with the therapy and give Dre a big hug from me.

Allegra

APRIL 27

9:04 a.m.

Stellina,

Are you getting sick? Why the exhaustion and insomnia? Do you feel okay?

Therapy's fucking hard, but you're right—I have to do the

work. Just wish there wasn't so much of it. We're currently wading through my bullshit. And there's so much, it's overwhelming. But, Kris—that's my therapist—is a good, patient guy. He reminds me of Dre. I'm going two times a week now.

I'll settle apartment shit with Levi and not bother you with the details. I'm glad the two of you have reconnected and are spending quality time together. He's a good man, your brother. One of my best fucking friends. Even when I want to deck him.

Yeah, Stellina, always better something than nothing.

How are the girls? How's work at the NGO? Are you working late nights? Is someone around to walk you to your car?

Let me know what you're up to. I miss you, little star. Talk soon.

Love,
Derek

I SEND OFF THE EMAIL. The little whoosh sound is comforting. At least Allegra will read my words, even if she can't listen to my voice. At least she'll know I'm still—fuck, always—thinking of her.

I crack my neck and stand from the butcher block island. Glancing around the brownstone, I miss the chaos it usually holds.

With Mav off sunbathing and Jameson fishing, it's eerily empty. I rub at the center of my chest, antsy. Having spent most of the night in the studio, I know I should crash.

But I don't want to sleep. I don't want to be alone any longer with my thoughts. My loneliness. My fucking self.

Pulling out my phone, I dial Dre.

He answers on the first ring. "What's good, man?"

"You hungry?"

Dre laughs. "Going out of your mind, huh?"

"That little diner in South Boston," I continue.

Dre sighs. "Yeah, brother. I'll meet you."

I grin. "Great. Half an hour?"

"See you there." Dre ends the call.

I breathe out a shaky exhale. Good man, Dre Ruiz, making sure I fill my idle time with something constructive. Like eating breakfast and having a normal conversation.

Like not obsessing over my father. Derek Madden.

Or my time with Simon and the bruises he left all over my body.

Or the loss of Allegra, and how it often feels like I'm internally bleeding, slowly dying. No one can fucking see it. And even if they could, would anyone give a shit?

My phone beeps with an alert and I sigh again.

Tomorrow is therapy.

Does this shit get any easier? Living, breathing, creating?

Does anything ever make any damn sense?

I bite the corner of my mouth and glance at the inbox on my laptop screen.

Allegra Rousell.

Her name, right there, in my inbox.

Live. Breathe. Create.

Apologize. Earn. Show up.

Do the fucking work.

Yeah.

I'm doing it for her. For me. For us.

Right now, I need to believe in that.

I need to believe in something.

TWO
ALLEGRA

"HE WON'T TAKE the fucking money," Levi swears and slaps down his returned check on the kitchen island.

I glance at Derek's name, note the amount, and sigh. "Forget it, then." I pick up the check and tear it in half.

"I'm not living in a place he paid for," Levi replies.

"We're moving," I remind him.

"I don't want his fucking money," my brother continues.

"I know," I say, agreeing. I don't want to take Derek's money either. But...I glance down at my still flat belly. For how long? When do pregnant women start to look pregnant? "Write me a check," I say.

Surprise crosses Levi's face. "You want the money?"

"Nope," I say. "But..." My hand protectively cups my lower abdomen. What is the baby? The size of a dust speck? Or a pomegranate seed? When a girl on Ivy's softball team learned she was pregnant last year, Mckenna told her about a newsletter that will send you your baby's weekly fruit size. I should sign up. "I'll put it in an account for..."

"The baby," Levi fills in the blank. Snapping his fingers

and pointing at me, he nods enthusiastically. "That's a great fucking idea."

"You'll have to swear less when he or she arrives," I point out, sitting on a barstool.

Levi snickers and moves to the cabinet to pull out peanut butter. "Want a sandwich?" he asks as he makes a pb and j.

I shrug. "Sure." Why not? I'm eating for two these days.

"How are you feeling?" Levi asks.

I shake my head. "Confused."

"Because of the baby? Or Derek?"

"Both." I drop my elbows to the island and plant my face in my hands. "And I'm fucking—"

"Swearing!"

"Tired. But can't sleep," I lament, looking back up.

Levi shoots me a sympathetic glance and slides a plate in front of me.

I pick up my sandwich and take a bite. "Thanks."

"You should tell him."

I huff, exasperated. "Through email?"

"Call him," Levi urges. "Allegra, Derek and I may hardly be speaking but..."

"But?" I pause, my sandwich halfway to my mouth.

"But he's one of my best friends."

"Funny. He said the same thing about you."

"And he deserves to know the truth."

"Maybe," I agree. Deep down, I know I need to share the news with Derek. But how? "I don't know what to say."

"How about, you're going to be a dad!" Levi announces, doing jazz hands like a pain in the ass.

"Or thanks for knocking me up," I deadpan.

Levi smirks. "He'll be on the next plane out here."

"I know," I agree. "That's partly why I'm not telling him."

Levi frowns. "You don't want to see him? Really? Because you've been mopey, and I don't think you can blame all of that on the baby."

"Hey!" I cup my stomach again. "I'm not blaming shit—anything—on my baby."

Levi pales. "I didn't mean it like—"

"And, no, I don't want Derek to come. One, it's too hard, okay? I love him. Am in love with him. I don't want him hanging around me just because I'm pregnant with his baby. I want him here because he loves me and is ready to be with me. Truly, as a partner. And two, he's doing well. Working through his own issues. I'm not derailing that until I have more news to tell him."

"Like, confirming this pregnancy with an actual doctor instead of a pee stick?"

"Exactly." I nod.

"And when is that appointment taking place?"

I sigh. "Two weeks."

"Did you tell the girls?" Levi takes a bite of his peanut butter and jelly.

I sigh again. "Not yet."

Levi grins even though it doesn't reach his eyes. "So, right now, I'm the only person in your circle of trust?"

I snort and toss a piece of crust at him. "Don't look so thrilled by that."

"I am, though. Thrilled. Relieved, even. I want you to trust me again, A."

"Yeah," I breathe out. "A lot of people want that." By people, I mean Derek, and Levi knows it.

"Hey." He reaches out and places his hand on mine.

"I'm here for you, okay? Whatever you need, I'm here. I got you."

"I know," I say softly. "Thank you for sorting out all of this." I gesture to the apartment we're moving out of tomorrow. Levi got us settled in a newer, bigger, two-bedroom place with more bells and whistles. "And for letting me take a step back from Beirut. I don't want you to feel—"

"A, stop with the money shit. I'm your brother. You showed up for me while I was in rehab. Let me show up for you. That's how we used to operate, remember?"

Begrudgingly, I smile. "Yeah, I remember."

"So, let's be us, again. We're doing this." He holds out his fist for me to bump.

I pretend like I'm considering his offer and Levi barks out a laugh.

Grinning, I tap my knuckles to his. "We're doing this."

My brother grins. "We're having a baby!"

I laugh and roll my eyes. "Don't say it like that. You don't need to feed any more gossip columns than you already are."

Levi snorts, his eyes gleaming. "True." Then, his gaze softens. "I'm proud of you, A. You're going to be one hell of a mom."

"I hope so," I say, thinking about our mother. She's a good woman but won't cross our stern, strict father. Even if it means losing Levi and me.

Glancing down at my invisible dust-speckled pomegranate seed, I heave out a sigh.

Even though this is the shock of a lifetime, I already know I'll pick my little fruit over everything.

Over my family. Over Derek. Even over myself.

The thought gives me a surge of confidence.

I can do this. I can be a good mom.

I can be enough to this beautiful surprise.

My miracle and my magic.

APRIL 29

4:24 p.m.

Derek,

Yeah, I feel okay. Just, adjustments. Transitions. You know how it goes.

Levi and I are moving into a new place tomorrow. I know you returned his check. I wish you didn't, but if you insist on being stubborn, I want you to know that I'm putting the money in a savings account. I don't have the energy for this to be a thing, but in the future, it can be.

I know it's tough. Wading through emotional things, trying to process them. It's funny (not really) but the person who probably can relate the most is Levi. Maybe you should reach out to speak with him about non-band things? Maybe he can even help?

In the meantime, I'm happy you're doing the work. I'm proud of you for showing up. I hope therapy, coupled with music, helps.

And I know for a fact that Dex is happy to speak with you and answer any questions you may have at any time. I don't know if it's too soon, but he really is a great guy. He could be a good resource for you, if you let him.

I'm going out to dinner with the girls tonight. It will be good to spend time with them. We've all been super busy. Mckenna's been accepted to the University of Boston Law School. She's over the moon and sorting out her move back to New England after graduation. Nova's smitten with the football player she started dating. And Ivy's busy with softball.

But, now that I'm back, I want to spend as much time with my friends as possible. Especially with graduation looming.

I hope you have a great week.

Allegra

I send the email before getting into the shower. I'm looking forward to dinner with my friends tonight even if I don't want to tell them the truth.

I'm pregnant. I'm having Derek's baby. And he doesn't know.

Shaking my hair out from the clip I had it pinned back with, I step beneath the hot stream of water. I close my eyes, tip back my head, and let the water wash away my exhaustion. My fear. My loneliness.

Since discovering I'm pregnant, nothing has changed. Other than feeling drained, I don't feel sick. There's no nausea or breast tenderness. There's no food aversions or dizziness.

Shouldn't I feel something...more? Shouldn't I feel connected and in tune with my dust-speck? Or blueberry? Or grape?

I didn't even sign up for the newsletter.

Rinsing the conditioner from my hair, I vow to get my shit together. Now that I'm not working at Beirut, I have more time. More time to plan, to figure out how I'm going to approach this pregnancy, to get prepared.

I step out of the shower and towel off. Then, I blow-dry my hair, apply some simple makeup, and dress in a long sundress and sandals.

First, I need to lean on my support system. That means letting my friends in on the truth.

Steeling my shoulders, I swipe up my car keys and purse. I can do this. It's going to be fine.

"Levi?" I call out as I leave my bedroom.

My brother's head pops up from the book he's reading on the couch.

I frown. "You're...reading?"

He shrugs. "Had a lot of time in rehab."

I squint at him. "Clearly."

He smirks. "Heading out?"

"Dinner with the girls."

"Good. That's good, A."

"Yeah," I agree, moving toward the door.

"You gonna tell them?" Levi's voice stops me in my tracks.

Turning to glance back at him, I nod. "I'm going to tell them."

His grin widens into a true smile. "Have fun."

I laugh. "Yeah. I'll try."

I don't admit that all of it—the having fun, the telling them, the needing support—would be a hell of a lot easier with a margarita in hand.

But I'm being a responsible adult.

I'm growing into a mother just as much as I'm growing my little fruit into a baby.

THREE
DEREK

"WHY DON'T you reach out to him?" Kris asks, leaning back in his chair and crossing one ankle over his opposite knee.

I sigh. "And say what?"

"Whatever comes to mind," my therapist replies reasonably.

I open and close my hand a few times, a restlessness running through my limbs. "I hate that he knows her. That she knows him."

"Allegra?"

I snort. "Yeah. Allegra."

"Because they have a relationship that you're not privy to? Or because Dex has become a fatherly figure to Allegra instead of acting like a father to you?" Kris prods.

I swear. "Both. I don't know," I growl, dropping my head back. Fuck, I hate this shit. I crack my neck and face Kris. "I don't want to begrudge her a male role model. A mentor. Whatever."

"Are you?"

"Out of all the fucking people in the world...it has to be him? Dex?"

Kris shrugs. "Maybe it's a good thing. A pathway. A common ground for you and Dex to connect on, if that's a relationship you'd like to develop."

"Don't tell me it's fate or some fucked-up shit like that."

Kris doesn't reply.

I arch an eyebrow.

He shrugs. "You'd have to believe in fate in order for that to make sense to you."

"I feel guilty," I admit.

"Why?"

"Because..." I throw out a hand. "Now that I'm connected to Dex, and Allegra knows it, she's not working at Beirut anymore. I'm sure she stepped back because of the... awkwardness of the situation. But I cost her a fucking mentor. All I ever do is cost that woman shit. Fuck her life up."

"Really? You don't think she'd keep the relationship with Dex going if it meant more to her than her loyalty, or connection, to you?"

My eyes snap to his. "What are you saying?"

"I'm saying that even though you and Allegra aren't speaking—"

"It's too hard for her," I remind him.

"You are communicating," he continues. "And it sounds like she's still prioritizing your feelings and your well-being in her life."

"And?"

"Have you considered that she's still betting on you? That she thinks you're worth the risk? That all isn't lost with her the way you think it is?"

"You're talking in riddles."

Kris grins. "Do you believe in those?"

"Fuck," I mutter and glance out the window.

"THANKS FOR MEETING ME," I say, taking the seat across from Dre.

Dre slides a coffee across the table. "Anytime. How was therapy?"

I snort. "Fucking work."

"Bet. You reach out to Dex yet?"

I glare at my friend.

He smiles. "Allegra?"

"Fuck off," I murmur.

Dre's smile widens. I take a swig of my coffee.

We're sitting at Java House. It used to be a regular place to hang out. A trendy coffee bar not too far from the brownstone.

But now, being here kicks up a wave of nostalgia.

"You interviewed her at that table." I flip my chin toward the empty space. In my head, I see Allegra, dressed in simple jeans and a button-down blouse, talking to Dre. I recall the expressive dance of her chocolate eyes and the way she spoke with her hands. His shoulders shook with laughter and when he glanced over at me, he hit the brim of his starter cap to let me see his expression. Dre let me know from the jump how much he liked my girl.

"Damn, Derek," Dre sighs. "You got it bad."

"I fucked up," I admit.

"So, call her."

"She doesn't want to talk to me. No..." I shake my head. "Scratch that. She doesn't want to hear my voice. Too painful."

Dre winces. "That girl's got a big fucking heart."

"Yeah."

"You broke it."

"Twice," I admit pathetically.

Dre glances down at his coffee mug, not saying anything since there's nothing to say.

"You know"—I shift in my chair, leaning over the table—"the entire time I was on tour, I fucking hated myself. Hated that I hurt her. Hated that I left her. But still, I thought I was doing right by her. Maybe it was delusional, but I truly thought, Allegra is better off pursuing her dreams without me and my bullshit."

Dre looks up, his gaze curious.

"And now..." I snort. "Now, I don't know what the hell I'm doing. I hate that I let her down, again. And I don't necessarily think she's better off without me. That's something Kris got into my head about," I admit. "I know I'm fucking nothing without her and yet..."

"What?"

"I don't know." I shrug. "I'm confused. My head is a mess. There's like this wall, a mental block, or something. I can't move past it, and I just feel stuck."

"So why don't you reach out to him?" Dre poses his question again.

"Derek Madden," I scoff. "Can you believe my mother named me after him? And never told me."

"Yeah, I can believe Judy did that," Dre murmurs quietly.

"And now she's dead," I spit out. "I'm so fucking angry at a woman who's not even around to hear it."

"You could tell me," Dre offers.

I scoff. "I'm in therapy, remember?"

Dre smirks. "Yeah, Kris is solid. What does he think you should do?"

"Reach out to him," I admit, not liking it any more coming from Kris than I do from Dre.

"You think he'd talk to you?"

"Allegra says he will."

Dre arches an eyebrow. "So, you and A are talking..."

"Via email," I huff. "Like fucking pen pals."

"Better than nothing."

"Yeah," I agree. "I don't even know what I'd say."

"I bet if you make the first move, he'll help you figure it out," Dre says seriously. Cautiously.

I narrow my eyes. "He didn't exactly win any parenting awards."

"He didn't exactly know he's a father," Dre shuts my shit down.

I heave out a sigh and hang my head. "My head is fucked, man."

"Yeah," Dre agrees. "But you're here, talking about it. Or meeting up with Kris. Or making music."

I look at him.

He smirks. "You're not getting blitzed, or fucking a nameless woman, or falling off the grid. You're dealing, Derek. In your own time and in your own way. But you are processing. You are trying. And you're doing your damnedest not to bring A down with you. Maybe you don't realize it. And maybe she can't see it. But I do. I know you, and the way you're acting right now...it's not in your nature. This isn't you reacting, it's you trying. Keep showing up."

"And doing the work," I murmur, repeating Allegra's words.

"Exactly," Dre says, smacking his lips together. He takes

another swig of coffee before knocking on the tabletop. "I gotta head out. Roll through this week?"

"Yeah," I agree. "I'm doing a music lesson on Friday."

Dre smiles. "Sarah and Jem will love that. Sarah is always asking for you. She's working on her own song now."

"Really?" I ask, happy to hear it. Sarah is an adorable kid. Pure hearted. The fact that I can make an impact on someone as good as her inspires some hope in myself.

"Come through and see for yourself."

"See you Friday," I commit.

Dre grins. "See you."

I watch as my oldest and truest friend exits the coffee shop. Then I lean back in my chair, stretch my legs before me, and think about what he said.

I'm trying. I'm not giving into my nature. I'm doing better.

Maybe I should reach out to him. My father.

Derek fucking Madden.

***

MAY 3

2:47 p.m.

Hey, Stellina,

How was your dinner with the girls? Congrats to Mckenna. Law school is no joke. I can see her doing it though. Living in the library and wearing those cardigans she rocks.

How's your new place? Did you and Levi settle in okay? Is he doing shit around the apartment or being a general slob and expecting you to clean up after him? Don't let him get away with that.

I'm doing good. Had another music lesson at the group

home on Friday. Sarah asked about you. She's songwriting now and to be honest, it's not half bad. She pours her heart into the words, little pieces of her soul and her hurt, and if she keeps it up, she could do something with it.

Dre asked me if I'd mentor her. I fucking laughed. Can you imagine me, mentoring someone? But the more I think about it...the more it doesn't seem so crazy. What do you think?

I've been thinking more about Dex. About reaching out to him. Fuck, it's weird. I thought about him—my dad—my whole life. To learn his identity at nearly thirty years old is a mind fuck.

What do we even talk about? What do I say?

It's awkward as hell and yet... I still have questions. I just don't know if I want the answers.

I miss you, little star.

Love,

Derek

I close my laptop and pick up my phone. Scroll through the messages. Delete the one from Mav's boy, Flip, asking if I want to party tonight. Blow up the image of Mav doing a flip off a fucking rock in the middle of the ocean.

Me: Don't crack your skull.

Mav: Scared I'll take your persona as edgy and closed off?

I snort. Fucking Mav.

Me: You can't pull it off. Your good looks are all you've got going for you.

Mav: (three middle finger emojis)

Me: How's Costa Rica?

Mav: Pura vida, baby. Come down for a visit?

Me: Can't.

Mav: Too busy brooding.

Me: Something like that.

Mav: Knock it off. It's been nearly a month. Pull yourself up by the bootstraps.

Me: And do what?

Mav: Call your dad. Talk to him. Get a fucking grip. Then, get your girl.

Me: Why does it sound so simple when you type it out?

Mav: 'Cause it is. Just a complicated mess in your messed-up head.

Me: Thanks, Mav.

Mav: Anytime.

Me: I was being sarcastic.

Mav: I was being truthful.

Mav: Call your father, Derek.

Mav: Then, come down here. Your soul will thank you for it.

I snort. Fucking Maverick makes everything seem easy and straightforward. He's the life of every party and by far every girl's favorite bandmate. He's likable and charismatic.

But not everything is black and white. I spend most of my time in the gray. And this shit with my dad is the most ambiguous thing in my life.

Still, with Allegra, Kris, Dre, and now Mav's voices, and wisdom, ringing in my ear, I open the email app on my phone.

Tapping out an email to Jess, I ask for Derek Madden's phone number. I know it's been sent via official correspondence on several occasions. Just because I have his number doesn't mean I have to call him.

Jess responds immediately with the digits.

I snort. I guess even she wants me to make the call, or she wouldn't have been so forthcoming with the information.

Do I call him?

Now or later? Should I send an email first to clear a time to talk?

I chuckle. It shouldn't be this stressful. A man talking to his dad shouldn't feel insurmountable.

I save his number in my contacts as Dex.

Kris is going to give me a gold star for this shit.

FOUR
ALLEGRA

"GOOD TO SEE YOU, A." Dex smiles warmly when I plop into the chair in front of his desk.

"You too, Dex." I grin and lean back in the seat. I glance around his soothing, nautical-themed office, and relax. While things are different between Dex and me, I still view him as a mentor. As a kind-hearted guy who looks out for my best interests and well-being.

He hands me an envelope. "Your last paycheck. You sure you're good? I know things are what they are, but you don't have to quit working here. Or you could, and I could still help you find a gig at another place in town."

"Thank you. Truly. I'm good. Levi and I moved into a bigger place and my brother's helping out now. But I appreciate the offer." I wave the envelope at him. "It's nice not to hustle so much at the moment. Spend more time on my classes and at the NGO."

"And seeing your friends."

"That too," I agree.

Dex nods but doesn't ask about Derek. Even though his gaze is curious, he was serious about not using me as a bridge to his son. I admire his resolve on the issue. I respect his decency. And because of that, I tell him the truth.

"Derek went back to Boston. We've been emailing but we're not together or anything. It's just...complicated."

Dex dips his head. "I'm sorry to hear that. About you guys not being in a relationship. How are you doing?"

I shake my head. "Not great. But not awful either."

His expression softens, his eyes filled with the wisdom of his years. With the shadows of his past. "I'm sorry, A."

"Me too. But," I say, standing, "I told him that you're open to speaking with him. That you'd like to answer any of his questions."

"Of course, I am. I'd love to."

"He hasn't reached out?"

"Not yet," Dex offers, his words wrapped in the kind of hope I wish I possessed.

It's got an undercurrent of belief I want to hold on to. The fact that Dex, a man who has endured so much, can maintain his hope fills me with a flicker too.

"I hope he reaches out soon," I say softly.

"I do, too." Dex stands and walks around the desk. He wraps me in a hug and gives an extra squeeze. "Don't be a stranger."

I pull back and smile. "I won't."

But even as I say the words, we both acknowledge that things between us have changed. There's a subtle shift in his expression that lets me know it's okay. That he doesn't expect me to confide in him anymore since doing so would feel like a betrayal to Derek.

"You're one hell of a dad, Dex," I mutter.

He barks out a laugh and shakes his head. "Any man would be lucky to have a daughter like you, A. Take care of yourself."

"See you," I say, lifting a hand in farewell.

I leave Beirut. As I walk to my car in the parking lot, a walk I've taken a hundred times, Dex's words play in my mind.

Any man would be lucky to have a daughter like you.

Why doesn't my dad feel that way? Why don't my parents care about me with the same edge of desperation I already feel for my blueberry?

I slip into the driver's seat of my car and flip the ignition. The backs of my thighs stick to the leather seats, and I blast the air conditioning, shifting my weight to get comfortable. As the car cools down, I pull up my contact list and dial the number for home.

Even though it hasn't felt like home in a long time, I haven't been able to change the name in my phone. Maybe I've got more of that delusional hope I accused Dex of hanging on to than I thought.

"Hello?" My father's voice comes through the line.

I gasp, not expecting it. He rarely answers the phone, leaving housework to my mother.

"Dad," I breathe out.

Silence fills the line for a long beat.

"Allegra?" he asks after a long moment.

"Yeah, I—"

The sound of the dial tone fills my ear as he disconnects the call.

Tears gather in the corners of my eyes at his rejection. I let out a shaky exhale and lean my head back against the headrest.

He will never open his arms, or his home, to me again. Why can't I accept that? I glance down at my blueberry. Is it because I'm about to become a mother that I can no longer justify my father's dismissal of me? Has impending motherhood already changed me?

No matter the reason, I can't comprehend how my father can be so cruel, so set in his beliefs, that there isn't any room for mine. He likes the idea of me—of having a daughter—more than me as an actual person, with thoughts and feelings and opinions. He doesn't want me the way he's supposed to. Not the way Buck and Dex cared for me.

And yet, a part of me keeps trying and hoping for a different outcome. Isn't that the definition of insanity?

The backs of my eyes tingle, and I blink faster.

"Ugh," I groan, fed up with my tears. Lately, it feels like I'm on an emotional roller coaster and I can't get off. A tear leaks out, but I brush it away before it can slide down my cheek. My father doesn't deserve my tears.

I glance down at my stomach and swipe my fingers over my belly button.

Any woman would be lucky to have you, I think to my little fruit.

This was never part of my plan, and I certainly don't feel ready to be a mother. But I also won't shun my child the way my parents have shunned me.

I can be better. Hope swells in my chest and I laugh.

Maybe Dex is onto something. Maybe I should adopt the wisdom he exudes.

Maybe I should keep hoping.

MAY 6

10:19 a.m.
Derek,
It's nice to hear from you but I hate how down you

sounded in your last email. As delusional, or hopeless, as it may feel, we should try to hang on to the possibility of good.

It may surprise us.

I love that Sarah is writing songs. I like the idea of you mentoring her even more. Didn't you have a music teacher who changed the game for you? Imagine being that for someone as good and bright as Sarah. Think about how much confidence she could gain from working with you.

My new place is good. It's light and airy, and Levi and I have settled into a routine. In a lot of ways, it's reminiscent of our childhood. He still takes ungodly long showers and doesn't put his dirty dishes in the dishwasher, but otherwise, he's a lot neater than I remember. He blames this on rehab—another positive outcome, in my book.

I called my house the other day. My dad answered. I held my breath. He asked if it was me and when I said yes, he hung up. Just disconnected the call. Cut me out of his life like I was a telemarketer.

I don't want to tell you what to do but I think you should reach out to Dex. You don't have to have a plan. You don't have to say anything. I already know he won't hang up on you.

Allegra

I send the email and lean back in my desk chair. Tears fill my eyes again and I blink them away. A whole day later and my dad's rejection still stings.

Why doesn't he care about me? Or love me? Why can't he be proud of the person I am?

I snort. There's no chance he'll embrace me now that I've conceived my little blueberry out of wedlock. He'll never acknowledge my baby as a legitimate Rousell.

For some reason, that hurts more than Dad's not acknowledging me.

My father's shortsightedness has cost him his relationship with both of his children and he's too myopic to see it. Hell, he probably doesn't acknowledge how much his actions have broken my mother's heart. How his obstinance also keeps her from having a relationship with her kids.

Dex and Derek have a chance at a real relationship. They can develop something meaningful. I know Derek's been hurt, repeatedly, and it's hard for him to trust another male. He's not going to automatically open up to Dex, but Dex isn't going to cut him off for not making the first step either. I hope Derek realizes the opportunity he has to know his birth father. I hope he doesn't squander it.

Shaking my head, a wave of dizziness washes over me. I reach out and clasp the back of my desk chair before moving to my bed. God, I'm tired. And emotional. Since learning I'm pregnant, my emotional state has been more affected than my physical being. My hand moves to my lower abdomen, and I cup my little fruit slice.

He or she isn't even fully formed and already, they've changed my outlook on life. Shifted my perspective. Switched up the lens through which I view the world, my relationships, and myself.

I rest my head on my pillow and snuggle under a blanket as sleep beckons. My limbs relax. The tension in my neck and shoulders seeps away. Derek's voice, sultry and singing, fills my mind, and I drift off to sleep.

I dream of a luscious garden. It's brimming with greenery, strong oak trees, and shady palm fronds. It's overflowing with fruit.

Bright and bold and beautiful.

Luscious and ripe and whole.

FIVE

DEREK

YOU VANISHED LIKE DAYBREAK,
Lost stars and forgotten night.
You haunt me like a shadow,
Clingy and relentless.
You haunt me like her.

YOU FADED LIKE A PHOTOGRAPH,
Broken memories and echoes of lost dreams,
You stalk me like my conscience,
Vile and futile,
You stalk me like pieces of her.

STARS DIE AND PLACES MERGE,
You turned my rebellion into a
Resentment that burns.
All-consuming and exhausting,
You hate me like her.

No, you hate me like me.

VANISHED DAY AND FADED MOMENTS,
  Broken memories and lost dreams,
  Stars burn too bright before they extinguish,
  And baby, I'm blazing for you.
  Yeah, you hate me like me.
  Girl, I fucking love you like you.

I LOVE *you more than the stars,*
  In spite of the loss,
  Beyond the destruction.
  You glow; I sear,
  Together, we're too bright
  To smother.
  So I'll suffocate on our hurt,
  And wrap you in my love,
  Because, Stellina, it's always been you.

I HOLD THE LAST NOTE, letting my emotion—the fucking pain and crushing guilt, the sinful shame and desperate hope—swell forward. It weaves through my tone, elevating my music into poetry. Giving Allegra the words, the explanation, I've held back for far too long.

"Fuck, Reign," the sound engineer, Pete, spits into the mic.

I open my eyes and manage a grin. "What do you think?"

"I think you just went platinum, motherfucker," he replies.

I snort and hang up my guitar. When I enter the room with my producer, Sam, he clasps my shoulder. "That was epic, Reign. That's your next single."

"That was personal," I admit.

He smirks. "Best kind of songwriting there is."

I sigh and grip the back of my neck. Vulnerability skates down my spine. My fingers twitch. Now that I let it all pour out, my tumultuous feelings and complicated thoughts, the mother who fucking haunts me, even from the grave, and the woman I don't deserve, even when I'm trying, I feel exposed. Raw and simultaneously overflowing and empty. I shake my head. "You think I should bring the band in?"

"Not on this," Pete murmurs.

Sam cuts him a look before glancing at me. "You want them in on this?"

"No," I decide. "This...it's personal. When they listen to it, they'll get that. They'll understand." The last thing I want to do is stir more shit up between my band members and myself. But this song, it's for Allegra. It's her song and every word sung, every note played, should be by me. And only me.

"Send it to them," Pete says. "I'm sending you the file. You should share it."

Sam nods. "See what they think. Let me know what you want to do."

"Okay," I agree. "Thanks, Pete. Sam. Appreciate you both coming in today."

"Anytime, Reign." Pete grins.

Sam smacks my shoulder again. "Get out of here. Get some sleep. You look exhausted."

"Yeah," I snort. "See ya around." Ducking my head, I slip out of the studio.

It feels weird, coming and going to this space without

the guys. But the past few weeks, the only thing filling the void in my soul and pausing the endless chatter in my mind is music. And this song...fuck, it's finally where I want it.

Before I can second-guess myself, I pull up the file Pete sent and drop it in a band group chat.

Me: Been working on something. What do you think?

Then, I head to the brownstone, take a shower, and pass out.

I wake up hours later to my phone ringing.

"Yeah?" I answer without checking the caller ID.

"You mean what you wrote?" Levi's voice pulls me up short.

I sit up in bed, my room darkened by dusk, and scrub the sleep from my eyes. My mind reels to catch up to his question. "You listened to the song." I clear my throat.

"Is it about my sister?"

"Yes," I admit. "Yes, it's for Allegra. And yeah, I mean it. I fucking love her, Levi."

He heaves out a long exhale. "Okay."

"Okay?" I sputter. What the hell does that mean? Okay, he likes the song. Okay, he doesn't hate the idea of me fighting for Allegra. Okay...what?

"Okay, I get it," he clarifies. "This whole time, part of me thought you were screwing with her. And then, the fact that you guys were...whatever...behind my back and I didn't see it, it bothered me. But in this song..." He trails off.

I work a swallow.

"Fuck, bro," Levi finally murmurs. "You laid your soul bare."

"Yeah," I agree, clearing my throat again. I don't know how to talk about this shit. I mean, I can confide in Dre and give my truths to Allegra, but within the band, it's always been easier to hold back. Let things out through the music, the lyrics, instead.

"You care about her," he determines.

"I love her," I clarify.

Then, Levi laughs. He chuckles and wheezes and fucking snorts.

"Why is that funny?" I bite out.

"It's not," he manages in-between his laughter. "It's... I'm relieved, Derek." The fact that he calls me Derek isn't lost on me. These past few months, I've been Reign.

Hearing him call me Derek again allows me to relax some, and I lean back against the pillows at my headboard.

"How's she doing?" I ask.

Levi's laughter fades. "She misses you," he admits.

"I miss her."

"Keep trying. Keep reaching out. Don't give up on her, Derek. She..."

"She what?" I pounce.

"She needs you more than she thinks she does. More than she realizes."

I frown at his word choice. "What's that—"

"I think you should release the song. Go at it solo but share it with our fans, with the world. It's a song that deserves to be shared and loved. Nice work, brother."

"Thanks, man," I say, appreciating his words.

"Yeah."

"We gonna record an album soon?" I ask. Levi already knows we're on deck to start recording, but I'm asking if we're going to do it as friends. As brothers. Instead of band-mates with a rift between us.

"I'm ready, Derek. Are you?" he tosses the ball back in my court.

I grin. "Been ready, mate."

Levi chuckles. "Good. I'll talk to you soon."

"Yeah. Speak soon."

Levi ends the call and I stare at the phone in my hand. Shaking my head, I slip from bed and pull on a pair of shorts and a hoodie. All those months of not speaking, or one-word responses to band business, of feeling like I lost my best friend, gone in an instant.

He accepts me. Forgives me. Doesn't hate me.

And hell, I've missed him.

My phone buzzes and I swipe it to check the group thread.

Mav: I fucking cried, you awful monster.

I laugh.

Jameson: This song is a hit, Derek. Release it.

Mav: Yeah, do you, bro.

Levi: Agreed.

Mav: Ooh, the Rousell brother has entered the chat! Does this mean the Cold War is...dare I say it? Melting...

Levi: Fuck off.

Jameson: Still hostile.

Mav: (three laughing face emojis)

Me: Mav, can I drop the track?

Mav: The sooner the better! Proud of you, Reign.

I don't respond to that because...what would I say? But some of the pressure in my chest eases at Mav's message.

Me: Keep you posted on it. When do you want to start recording?

Jameson: Two weeks?

Mav: Boston or LA?

Levi: Can we start in LA? A and I moved into a two-bedroom and...things are going well here.

Jameson: That's good, man. Sure, LA it is.

Me: I'll hit up Hendrix to schedule studio time.

Mav: Sweet! See you soon, bitches!

Me: You are such a fucking girl sometimes.

Mav: Says my all-time favorite biotch.

Rolling my eyes, I chuckle. Fucking Mav.

But in two weeks, we start recording. I glance at the notebook on the end of my bed. It's already filled with song lyrics and ideas. Energy hums through my veins, my fingers itching to get to work. To write more songs and make great music.

But first, I'll drop a single. Stellina's song.

I scroll through my contacts and pull up Sam's number. Then, I plop into a chair and give him a call.

MAY 8

7:52 p.m.

Derek,

I got an interview! Can you believe that? It's for a position with the NGO I'm volunteering at, serving homelessness in the greater LA area. I really hope it pans out.

My interview is next week. It's crazy to think I'm graduating in a few weeks but even crazier to know that I might have full-time employment lined up by then.

Ha! Stop worrying about me and the NGO. The area is well-lit, and I am perfectly capable of walking to my car at night. If I get the job, I'll be logging more hours there anyway.

Since it's not an official job offer and I'm nervous, I haven't said anything to Levi or the girls yet but... I wanted to tell you.

Hope you're having a good week,

Allegra

Her email brings a smile to my face, and I quickly tap out a reply.

May 8

7:58 p.m.

CONGRATULATIONS, STELLINA!

I'm confident that you will rock your interview and get the job! When is it? I bet they hire you on the spot!

Let me know as soon as they send you the official word, but baby, there's no doubt you're meant to do big, meaningful things. I'm proud of you, Allegra. And even happier that you shared this news with me first. I'm fucking gloating about it.

Are you excited for graduation?

You made my week!

Love,

Derek

THE REST of the week passes quickly. Sam wants to get the track finalized as soon as possible. I reach out to Claire Merrick to do some design work for the cover. I spend my mornings writing, my afternoons working, and a few evenings hanging with Dre at the group home.

My time there is met with warm hugs, peals of laughter, and the bright eyes of my best pupil, Sarah. Sitting with her, creating music, transports me to my childhood. To sitting in my music teacher's classroom, the subtle scent of glue and chalk, and fiddling with the strings of the guitar he gave me. Hanging with Sarah and seeing her progress motivates me to keep working on my lyrics for the upcoming album.

I'm adding the finishing touches to a new verse when my phone rings.

As soon as I note Levi's name on the screen, I drop my pen and close my notebook. Now that we exchanged a heart-to-heart, and he understands my true intentions toward Allegra, things shifted back into place. We're friends again in that easy and effortless way from before.

"What's good?" I answer.

"Derek," Levi rushes to say my name.

My fingers flex on my phone. A current of fear zaps through my system at the worry in his tone. "What's wrong?"

"Fuck, man. You gotta come. You need to be here."

"What's going on?" I repeat, already standing. My eyes scan my room for my wallet and keys.

"It's Allegra, man," Levi's voice cracks.

My blood runs cold, and I freeze. The back of my neck ices over and my lungs constrict as I try to pull in air. "What about Allegra?"

"Fuck," he swears again.

Each second that passes causes my blood pressure to rise until I'm certain I'm going to explode. Panic races through my veins and my fingers tremble as I toss some underwear and T-shirts into a backpack.

"Levi!"

"She's on her way to the hospital. Come now. I gotta go. I'll text you the info." He hangs up.

My stomach clenches and a wave of heat burns through my body before drenching it in ice-cold fear. "Fuck!" I roar.

What the hell happened?

Is she okay? What hospital?

What the fuck!

I swing my backpack over my shoulder and lift my phone to my ear. Barking out orders, I line up a private jet to take me to LA, ASAP. Then, I slide into the back seat of an Escalade and head to the private airport. The entire time, I chant meaningless prayers I've never believed in.

But fuck, do I want to have faith in them—in something —right now.

SIX

ALLEGRA

"I WAS GOING to see my doctor for a normal checkup," I say again to the nurse with the kind eyes.

"I know," she replies sympathetically. "And it's a good thing you did, or she wouldn't have diagnosed the pregnancy as ectopic. It's best to know this as early as possible."

I nod, even though her words don't make sense to me. I was supposed to confirm my pregnancy today, to learn what type of fruit my baby is, and to determine the due date.

I wasn't supposed to learn that my pregnancy isn't viable. That it ended before it really started. I wasn't supposed to spend hours waiting in the ER, panicked, and mentally agonizing over the dangerous outcomes of an ectopic pregnancy if I don't terminate it today.

"Am I having surgery?" I wonder. I think I've asked this question already but...my thoughts are all over the place. My head feels half underwater. It's as if I'm hearing everyone's voices through a long tunnel.

I hear their words, but I can't process them.

The empathy in their expressions though, that hits me like a boulder of emotion lodged in my throat.

Today is painful instead of beautiful.

And I'm more scared than I've ever been in my life. Each hour in the ER waiting room, watching as more pressing emergencies were handled, had me teetering on the brink of a full-blown panic attack.

What if my fallopian tube bursts? What if my doctor was wrong and my little fruit slice could defy the odds, and live? What if, over and over and over again.

Levi paced the private waiting area, his anger rising with each passing second. He spent the last hour glued to his phone, calling in favors to get my treatment expedited. But, since the Covid pandemic, the hospital has been short-staffed. The operating rooms have been occupied around the clock with backlogged surgeries in addition to incoming emergencies. The system of care has started to buckle.

Finally, they called my name. Levi helped me up from my chair, his face pale, his eyes hard with frustration and pain.

"I'll be right here," he told me, pointing to his chair.

I nodded and followed the nurse with the kind eyes.

Looking at me now, she gently replies, "The doctor will be in to discuss those options with you."

"Is my brother still here?"

"He's in the waiting room with some women...your friends?" She makes a guess.

I nod. Of course, Kenny, Ivy, and Nova showed up.

"And the baby's father?" the nurse questions, glancing at her notepad.

My heart swells and stutters. Derek's here? How does he even know? Who told him? How is—

"An Ethan Dresden," the nurse continues.

My hope plummets. My hands twist together, and I shake my head. "He's a friend too."

"Oh," she murmurs, her eyes flicking to mine. At the understanding in them, tears prick the corners of my eyes. "Well, you have some wonderful friends."

"Yeah," I mutter. "I'm a lucky girl."

A fortunate woman with no baby and no baby daddy.

The nurse places a gentle hand on mine. "The doctor will be right in."

"Okay," I agree.

She leaves and I glance around the hospital room. It's sterile and severe. Devoid of color. I sigh and close my eyes, rest my head back against the pillow. The hospital gown is stiff and scratchy against my skin.

I debate if I should ask Levi or Kenny to come back to keep me company. But I don't feel like talking. Tears push forward, filling my eyes. A few leak out underneath my eyelids and splatter onto my cheeks.

Ugh. I wipe them away. I don't feel like crying either. I'm so damn tired of sobbing.

A light knock sounds on the door. "Allegra Rousell?" The doctor, a young, attractive man, enters the room.

I lift a hand. "You found me."

One side of his mouth lifts in a smile but his eyes are serious. Thoughtful and sincere. "I'm Dr. Davis. How are you feeling?" he asks.

They really have great bedside manner at this place.

"Confused," I admit.

Dr. Davis nods. He moves to stand at the edge of my bed and stacks his folders against the foot railing. "That's understandable. I'm sure you weren't prepared for the news you received."

"Is anyone ever?"

"No." He shakes his head. "According to your ultrasound, your fallopian tube hasn't ruptured. In order to save the tube, and give you a greater chance at future pregnancies, I'd like to avoid surgery if possible."

"Can we do that?" I wonder.

He nods. "Yes. There's a medication we can try. It's offered via injection, and it will stop the fetus from growing. It's less invasive than surgery although it requires you to come back frequently for labs, to make sure the HCG levels are decreasing. If not, a second injection is required, although one usually does the trick. What do you think?"

I glance at the young doctor. He's older than me but I'd guess younger than Derek. He's good-looking and compassionate. He gives off "emotionally-available" vibes the same way Derek exudes an edgy "fuck-off" demeanor.

Objectively, I know an ectopic pregnancy can happen to anyone.

But in this moment, I wonder if hot Dr. Davis and the gorgeous significant other I envision him with, would find themselves in this position. Or am I here because of all the stupid shit I did? Did my acting out, being irresponsible and careless, bring this on?

"This isn't your fault," he murmurs, as if reading my thoughts.

"What if it's karma?" I blurt out.

Dr. Davis shakes his head. "It's not. These things happen and they can't be explained. It's just one of those things, but it doesn't mean you can't go on to have a healthy pregnancy in the future. If that's what you want."

"I don't know what I want," I admit.

"You don't have to know. You're twenty-two years old."

"Yeah," I agree, feeling another pesky tear land on my cheek. I flick it away.

"Is there anyone you'd like me to call back to be with you?" he offers.

I shake my head. "There's—"

"Allegra!" The door to my room flies open. The doorknob hits the wall and the door slams back, almost violently, before a tattooed hand with a snake catches it. Derek enters the room and immediately sucks up all the oxygen.

Dr. Davis turns toward him, a frown marring his face.

Derek doesn't even see him. In two strides, he's next to me. His knees hit the floor beside my bed and before I can form words, my hand is enveloped by his.

His eyes—bleeding concern and regret—bore into mine. "Fuck, Stellina, why didn't you tell me?" His voice is hushed and broken. Cracked concrete and crushed flowers.

Dr. Davis clears his throat. Derek ignores him. He finds my eyes over Derek's head. "I'll give you a few minutes."

I nod and watch as Dr. Davis slips from the room. The door closes with a soft snick, and I force my gaze back to Derek's.

"Why?" Derek repeats.

"I don't know," I admit.

His eyebrows knit together, and his eyes scan mine. What's he searching for? What does he hope to see?

I stare back but I'm not sure what my facial expression conveys.

Emotions swirl through me. Rapid and intense. There's too many—all conflicting—to settle on one.

A part of me is relieved that Derek's here. Another part hates that I want—no, need—him to be present.

And fuck, the guilt is intense. It's a boulder rocking in the pit of my stomach. Did I cause this? Will this outcome into existence?

Then, there's the overwhelming sadness of it. I feel broken and lost and empty. I feel bereft of hope. This wasn't supposed to happen. Not before me, Derek, and our little fruit slice, had a chance to hope and dream and be fucking whole.

"Allegra," Derek murmurs.

"Hm?" I shake my head.

"Talk to me, baby," he begs. "Please. Tell me something."

"Dr. Davis doesn't think it's karma."

A bewildered expression crosses Derek's face. "Of course, it's not fucking karma. This isn't your fault, beautiful. If anything"—the color leeches from his cheeks—"it's mine."

"No, it's not," I reject the stupidity of his statement.

He swears softly. "How do you figure? I didn't even fucking know. I wasn't even here."

"You're here now," I point out.

"Yeah. We're together now." He squeezes my fingers.

I don't say anything. Because I know he means beyond this moment. Derek still wants the happily-ever-after and right now, I don't feel hopeful about the future. Mine or his or ours.

Right now... "I'm tired."

"I know," he says. "What did the doctor say?"

I tell him about the injection.

"Is that what you want?" he asks.

I shrug. "Seems like the better option."

"Okay." Derek nods. "Then, let's do it. Together. Whatever you need, Allegra, I'm here. You're not in this alone." He dips his head to catch my eyes. They flare. "Yeah?"

"Yeah," I agree, squeezing his fingers back.

"I love you," he swears, as if it's a pledge.

"I know."

"And I'm right fucking here, okay?"

"Okay," I whisper.

Dr. Davis knocks lightly before re-entering the room.

"Do you have any questions, Allegra?" He keeps his gaze trained on me.

I shake my head.

Then, Dr. Davis turns to Derek. "I'm Dr. Davis. And you are...?"

"Derek." Derek stands and offers his hand. Dr. Davis shakes it. Derek's eyes find mine. "The father," he announces.

Dr. Davis nods. "It's good you could be here. For her."

"Yeah. I'm not going anywhere either," he repeats it again. Defensive as hell.

The nurse re-enters. She gives Derek a warm smile before helping position me.

"Where do you give the injection?" Derek frowns.

"In the buttocks," the nurse replies.

I glance at Derek and bite my bottom lip. It shouldn't be funny. Fuck, it's not funny. But when my eyes meet his and I see the humor that fills his irises, it lightens the load I'm carrying.

I reach for him and he's there, holding my hand, grasping my arm, and staring at me intently.

Our eyes hold the entire time. Derek gives me his strength, his affection, his love, and it makes the process emotionally bearable. A small voice sounds in my mind, reminding me that I'm going to be okay. That I'm going to get through this. Staring into Derek's steadfast, dark brown eyes, I know it's true. I relax slightly and pull in a breath as the needle pierces my skin. After the injection, I'm helped back into the bed.

"Just rest for a little," Dr. Davis advises. "If you're

feeling well, we'll get you discharged within the hour. Do you have anyone to help you at home?"

"Yes," I say. "My brother, Levi, is—"

"I'll be with her," Derek cuts me off.

I gasp, my eyes snapping to his.

"You have me," he bites out. His eyes glare at me. *We're in this together.*

I sigh, not bothering to respond.

"Okay," Dr. Davis says after a beat. "Do you have any questions for me?"

I shake my head.

Derek clears his throat.

Dr. Davis glances at him.

"Will this affect her ability to have children? In the future?" he asks.

My mouth drops open as I stare at him. Who is Derek to ask questions like that? Why is he taking an active role in this painful, awkward moment when I've been on my own for the past few weeks?

You should have told him, my mind whispers.

I close my eyes and turn my head.

"If she's responsive to the injection, and we're able to save the fallopian tube, Allegra should be able to have healthy pregnancies in the future. But an ectopic pregnancy also increases the chances of having a future ectopic pregnancy by 10–15%."

My eyes fly open.

Derek's staring straight at me, his gaze darker than a starless sky, his jaw clenched. His body is tense, with his hands curled into fists and his shoulders rolling forward. He snaps his eyes to the doctor. "Is there anything specific I should know for Allegra's care?"

"Nurse Anna"—he points to the sweet nurse—"will come round with all the care instructions," Dr. Davis replies.

Anna pats my hand sympathetically.

Derek nods. "Thanks." His tone is clipped.

Dr. Davis looks at me. Tries to smile encouragingly. "I'll get your discharge paperwork going. Check in on you soon, Allegra."

"Thanks, Dr. Davis," I reply.

He leaves and Anna follows.

Derek grips the side of my bed railing, his tattoos rippling over his knuckles. "Move in with me," he says. "I'll take care of you."

"Derek," I sigh. I don't want to have this conversation right now. I don't want to make decisions. I have no clue what the hell I want, but I do know that I'll reject any option currently presented.

"It's okay," he murmurs, brushing my hair away from my forehead. "We don't have to talk about this now. Close your eyes, Stellina. Get some rest. I'll be right here." He sits in the chair beside my bed.

I nod and allow my eyes to close. Rest my head. Beg for sleep to claim me.

It doesn't take long. I'm exhausted and drained and so fucking sad.

Sleep pulls me under, and I dream about that garden. But this time, it's not luscious and green and bursting with color.

It's dead. Dark and bleak and black and white. Shades of gray. It's...empty. Barren.

In the garden, I plop down on a mushroom, plant my face in my hands, and sob. But even my tears don't provide nourishment to the soil. My pain doesn't make anything grow.

Instead, the roots of the trees twist and knot. The branches dip and wither. The garden grows cold.

And still, I cry.

SEVEN

DEREK

SHE LOOKS EXHAUSTED. Beautiful.

Fucking heartbreaking.

I turn away from the hospital bed swallowing up my sweet Stellina. And fuck, I want to roar. Or run.

Restless energy thrums through my veins. It gathers and builds, rising to the base of my throat, where it threatens to suffocate me. I swallow it back. There's no place for me to put it. There's no place for it to go.

I step closer to the window and glance outside. It's sunny and warm, with people milling about on the street below. Oblivious, lost in their thoughts, maybe even happy.

None of them realize that staring down at them, prowling on the edge of a precipice, is a caged lion. A fucking fallen star.

I blow out an exhale and drag a hand through my hair.

I was going to be a father. A fucking dad.

My stomach twists as my chest tightens. I pinch the back of my neck, as if to hold me tethered to this moment. This thought. The idea is almost too ludicrous to believe. I don't know the first thing about being a parent. The handful of serious connections—commitments—I've had, have ended in disaster. Dre. The band. Allegra.

And sure, they're all still in my life in some capacity, but I can't pretend that their knowing me hasn't fucked them up in some way.

Sarah's face, her ginger corkscrew curls, and laughing eyes flicker to mind.

My little protégé is the only person who still looks at me with open trust. Without a layer of unease.

I frown. Is that what having a kid would be like? Would they love me—unconditionally—until I fucked them up? And then what, would they despise me?

It's a mind fuck, that's what it is. And yet, as much as I want to run and roar and drop to my knees and beg someone—maybe that faceless God I pleaded with on the flight here—for answers, I don't. I turn away from the window and the sunshine and the oblivious people who are happier than me, and drop into the chair beside the bed.

I stare at the gorgeous beauty I won't ever deserve, and something inside of me shifts. Settles. I'm staying for her and for the first time in my life, it feels right. I don't second-guess it. I don't wonder *what if?*

I know that I'm here, right now, for however long it takes, because she needs me. And hell, I've never not needed her.

The curve of Allegra's cheeks, the flutter of her long eyelashes as she dreams, the purse of her lips, she's my everything. I love her. And it hurts to know that she's hurting. That our baby—a baby I didn't know existed—isn't in our future.

Why didn't she tell me? How could she know that she was pregnant—with our baby, my baby—and tell Levi and her friends before me?

Did she think I wouldn't show up? Or care?

Did she think she couldn't trust me with the news?

The realization that I had no fucking clue, would still have no idea, if Levi didn't call me twists my stomach. I feel sick about it and yet, there's no place to put that anger either.

I can't pile it on my Stellina. Not when she was scared and confused and uncertain. Not when I took off, unable to handle my own shit, and left her behind.

But understanding our unique situation doesn't make me feel better. If anything, I feel fucking worse. Bitterness coats my tongue and explodes in my gut.

I was going to be a father. I roll my lips together to keep from smiling at the thought. I don't deserve to fucking smile.

Besides, the idea of becoming a dad should scare me more than it is.

Is it because it's no longer happening?

Or is it because I know, deep down, that with Allegra as our child's mother, there would be hope. There would be sunshine and happiness and magic. There would be a slice of that oblivious happy-go-lucky outlook I crave as much as it annoys me.

I reach forward to brush my fingers through her hair. My Stellina. Even in sleep, she glows. And in the darkest of days, the bleakest of moments, her spirit shines.

No, I'll never deserve her. But I'm done running.

For her, I'll stay and wait forever.

"HOW IS SHE?" Levi knocks gently on the door.

"Still sleeping," I admit, glancing at my watch. "Dr. Davis offered to discharge her about forty minutes ago but..." I shrug, glancing at her sleeping form. Allegra must be physically exhausted and mentally drained. The rest is good for her.

"Let her sleep," Levi murmurs. "God knows she was in that waiting room for too fucking long." He moves to the window and leans against it, staring at me.

"What?" I ask.

Levi lifts his chin. "How are you holding up?"

"Fuck," I bark out, unprepared for his question. I grip the back of my neck. "My head's a mess."

Levi nods. "To be expected."

"Is it?" I challenge.

"This would fuck with anyone, Derek." His tone holds more compassion than I deserve.

I lean forward in my chair, dropping my elbows to my knees. Glance up at him. "Why didn't she tell me?"

"She was scared," he admits.

"That I'd—"

"It wasn't only about you," he cuts me off.

I sit up straight. If it wasn't about me, then who the hell was it about?

Levi smirks. "Not everything is about you, ya know?"

I flip him the middle finger.

His smirk widens into a grin before he shakes his head. "She was processing. I think she was torn, to be honest. On one hand, it was this total curveball. She's not ready to be a mom. She doesn't have a plan. But part of her was hopeful. Happy. I don't think she knew what to think, and until she had a handle on her emotions about it, she didn't want to tell anyone."

"She told you," I point out.

He rolls his eyes. "Not much of a choice when I'm living with her."

"She told her friends," I remind him.

"We had to talk about that. And they would've thought something was really wrong if she suddenly begged off margaritas."

"Fair," I begrudgingly admit.

"Mate, she didn't want to overwhelm herself any more than she already was. And, let's be honest, you weren't here, and you were working through legit *things*. Tell me if the positions were reversed, you'd call my sister up and drop a bomb on her fucking head when she's already in the deep end, desperately trying to make it to the shallows?"

I lean back in my chair and think over Levi's words. "I would've come back." I sound defensive.

"I know," Levi gives me the out. "I think she knew too. She wanted to confirm the pregnancy first. It was important to her to hear the heartbeat on her own, and know this was happening. For real."

"What happened?"

"When she went in for the appointment, the doctor discovered the pregnancy wasn't viable."

"Ectopic," I spit the word, hating it, even though up until a few hours ago, I didn't even know what it meant.

"Yeah. Ectopic," Levi repeats. "I called you as soon as I hung up with her."

"I got on a private plane."

"Figured. I didn't expect you to be here this quickly." He shakes his head. "Or for her to have to wait so damn long."

"I didn't think I'd make it here in time for whatever the hell was going down," I admit, recalling my desperate prayers.

"Glad you did."

I nod and look at my friend. Really look at him, so he

can see the resolve in my expression, read my intent. "I'm not leaving her."

He stares back at me. "Good."

"I want her to live with me."

Levi scoffs. "That's between you and my sister."

"Yeah," I agree, straightening in my chair and hunching forward. I glance up at my bandmate. "But would that mess with your recovery? If Allegra was at my place and you were living solo?" As much as I want Allegra in my place, in my fucking bed, in my arms, I know how hard Levi's worked to get to where he is. I don't want to mess with that either.

Levi looks surprised. "I, uh, I don't know. I'm taking things one day at a time. Hitting up meetings, sometimes twice a fucking day," he admits.

I nod. "Can't be easy."

"It's not." Levi sighs and steps toward me. "Derek, nothing worth a goddamn thing is easy. Relationships, even the one with ourselves, are the hardest. You want something meaningful in your life? Then you need people. Connections. My sister knows that more than anyone, and she knew it early on too. I'm glad you're not going anywhere. She deserves someone to put her first, and you and I are finally giving her what she gave us for a long time."

"Support?" I guess.

He smiles. "Love, you dumb fuck."

I laugh. Levi chuckles.

He tips his head toward the door. "Go take a walk."

I shake my head. "Not leaving, remember?"

He flips me the finger. "I want a minute with my sister. Go. Take a piss. Grab a coffee. Give me a few minutes."

I sigh. "All right," I say, standing. "I'm going to grab a

coffee. Make some phone calls. I'll be back in a few to check on her. You need anything?"

"Nah," he says, sitting down in my vacant chair. "I'll message you if she wakes up."

"Thanks," I say. I move toward the door and turn back to watch Levi lean closer to his sister's side.

For months, maybe years, Allegra yearned for a real relationship with Levi. It's good to see them healing old wounds, to witness them showing up for each other.

They remind me that I can right old wrongs, too.

Stepping into the hallway, I hit up Hendrix to arrange for studio time. I talk to Sam back in Boston. I check in with my manager, Jess, and run a few things by Aiden, my lawyer.

Then, I grab a coffee. I go outside, step into the sunshine, and move through the warm breeze until I find a bench.

I plop down. Smile and say congrats to a beaming woman who announces that she just became a grandmother. She's fucking happy.

I pull out my phone and dial.

"Hello?" He answers on the second ring.

"Dex?" I say. Clear my throat. "It's Derek."

"Derek." If he's surprised, he doesn't show it.

His calm demeanor sets me at ease.

"How's it going?" Dex asks after a beat of silence.

I bite the corner of my mouth to keep from—what? Laughing? Or maybe crying? I don't know what the fuck it is, but a bubble of emotion, a fucking squall, rises inside of me. Crashes down on top of me. I heave out a shaky exhale. "Not great," I admit.

"You wanna talk?" he offers. And it's such a fucking dad

thing to say, devoid of the judgement I expected. The judgement I'm used to. I fight back tears.

"Can we?" I nearly sob.

"Hell yeah," Dex replies. "You up for a Coke and a burger?"

I nod, before remembering he can't see me. "That'd be great. Is tomorrow okay? Lunchtime?" I don't want to take off now. Not until Allegra is settled and comfortable in her own bed.

"Lunch sounds good. I'll text you the details to a spot I like. Noon?"

"Noon," I confirm. "I'll, uh, I'll see you, Dex."

"Yeah," he mutters. Then, "Hey."

"Yeah?"

"I'm glad you called, Derek."

New emotions swell in my chest. Fuck, what the hell is happening to me?

I clear my throat again. "Same. See you tomorrow." I disconnect before I do something insane, like fucking sob.

I stand and pace in front of the hospital for a few minutes.

Thoughts swirl in my mind. Emotions I'm unfamiliar with wrestle for space in the cavity of my chest. My fingers tremble with that restless need to create.

I pull in a deep, cleansing breath. Let it out.

Look around at the people milling around and smile.

Hell, maybe I can be happy too.

EIGHT
ALLEGRA

"DO YOU NEED ANYTHING?" Levi asks.

"How about a magazine?" Derek offers.

"Or a juice?" Mav suggests.

"Are you cold?" Jameson tosses in.

I stare at the members of The Burnt Clovers and wrack my mind for why they're all here, standing in Levi's and my living room, staring at me like I'm a fragile piece of china about to break.

"I'm fine," I manage.

Levi frowns. Derek's jaw tics. Mav looks at me skeptically. Jameson shrugs.

I smile. "Did you all come into town for...me?" I guess.

"Of course," Mav replies.

"But you were in Costa Rica," I point out.

"And now I'm in LA." He shrugs, like it's no big deal.

"Thank you," I tell Mav and Jameson. Opening my arms, they both step forward for a hug. Mav, willingly, since he's a hugger. Jameson, hesitantly, because we're not nearly as close as me and Mav. Still, I give him a tight squeeze.

When they release me, Derek's at my side. He gently

takes my elbow and guides me toward my room. "Come on. Let's get you into bed."

Normally, I'd protest. But he's right; I need rest. My mind has alternated between a constant stream of thoughts and threatening to shut down completely. My body aches, an emptiness spreading through my limbs that I know reflects the loss I feel.

I wave to the guys and move toward my bedroom.

When we cross the threshold, Derek gently swings me into his arms and kicks my bedroom door closed behind him. He settles me in the center of my bed and moves toward my dresser, pulling open a few drawers.

"Top right," I say.

He pulls open the drawer and pulls out my pajamas. A soft T-shirt I swiped from him and a pair of sleep shorts. When he spots the T-shirt, recognition flares in his gaze. His eyes soften as he turns toward me.

He drops the pajamas next to my hip and grasps the hem of my shirt. "Up."

I put my arms in the air and let him peel my shirt off my frame. He doesn't spend time checking me out. Instead, his touch is careful, his eyes averted from my chest. He pulls his T-shirt over my head, and I pop my arms through the arm holes.

"Lie down," Derek murmurs, his voice huskier than it was a moment ago.

I do. My eyes close as he pops the button on my denim shorts.

For a heartbeat, I recall the times he undressed me. The desperate and frantic moments of him taking me to bed. Of our mouths clashing, our lips savoring.

"Lift."

My hips rise from the bed. Derek rolls my shorts off. He

works my sleep shorts up my legs and straightens them on my hips. Then, he pulls back my comforter and gets me settled, my head resting against propped pillows.

When I'm tucked in, he perches on the edge of my bed. "Are you hungry?"

I shake my head.

He tries again. "Thirsty?"

"No."

Derek takes my hand and laces our fingers together. "I'm glad you're home."

"I'm glad you're here," I admit.

He nods. "Me too. I want you to move in with me, Allegra. I know this is a fucking lot, but I want to take care of you. I'm all in this with you and I want us to do it, whatever the fuck it is, together."

I exhale and sink deeper into my pillows. I knew this was coming; Derek mentioned as much at the hospital. But does he mean it? Is he really going to stay? And do I want to move?

"I like my place," I admit. "I just got settled here."

"I know." Still, his eyes hold mine and I note the pleading ring around his irises.

"Plus, my brother is here so..." I trail off, not wanting to speak of Levi's recovery with Derek. Whatever Levi chooses to share with his bandmates is his business.

But I wouldn't feel right bouncing when he's fresh out of rehab to appease Derek's ego.

"Right," Derek says, surprising me. "I understand."

"You do?" I sputter.

He laughs. "Yeah, babe. I get it. I just want you to understand that I'm not going anywhere. And I want to be the one to look after you. Not Levi or fucking Mav."

I snort. "Okay," I agree.

"Okay," he says. "Want to sleep for a bit?"

I yawn and snuggle deeper in my pillows. "Want to watch a movie?" I know I won't make it too long into the film until sleep claims me, but right now, I don't want to be alone. I want to feel the warmth of Derek's body next to mine in bed. I want to have some reassurance that he means what he says.

That he's going to take care of me. Be here as I navigate these strange feelings that change from one moment to the next. Help me through this wallowing sadness that feeds on every cell in my body.

I feel it, but I can't show it. I want to process it, but it's daunting.

"I'd love to," Derek says. He kicks off his shoes and slips into the bed next to me. Underneath the covers, his hand finds mine. Our fingers thread together. With his spare hand, he flips on my television and navigates to Netflix.

"I called Dex," he mentions out of nowhere.

I turn to look at his profile. "You did?"

"Yeah."

"And?"

"We're going to have lunch tomorrow. At noon."

I smile. Squeeze his hand twice in encouragement. "That's wonderful. I, I'm proud of you, Derek."

Derek's head rolls toward mine. He stares deep into my eyes. Squeezes my hand back once. "I wouldn't have been able to do it without you, Allegra."

"That's not true," I say softly.

"Yeah. It is. I want to be better for you more than I want it for myself. I want to be the kind of dad a kid could be proud of. Not now," he rushes to explain, given our loss. "But one day."

"You will be," I whisper. His words play every emotional note in my body.

"I hope so," he counters. He settles on a show. "How about this matchmaking show?"

I bite my bottom lip. "That's perfect."

"I figured you'd like it," he mutters as he presses play.

Our heads tip toward each other as we watch the candidates on the show introduce themselves.

Before the first two candidates make it to their first date, I'm asleep.

But Derek's touch, the weight of his fingers against mine, the scent of his cologne, follows me into sleep. And it soothes something deep inside my soul. He brings me peace and I swim in it, feeling like I can breathe deeply for the first time in days.

———

I DON'T KNOW how many hours pass, but when I wake up, I'm alone in my bedroom. My throat is dry, and I feel groggy. It's dark outside.

I swing my legs to the edge of my bed and shit, is that blood? I study my sheet before glancing at my sleep shorts. Fuck. It's blood.

I move toward my bathroom to get cleaned up. The doctor said this would happen and yet, I wasn't thinking clearly. I change my clothes, slap a pad into my underwear, and move to change my sheets.

My bedroom door swings open, and Derek enters. "You're awake," he says brightly. Noting the blood, he frowns. "What's wrong? Are you okay? Do you feel—"

"It's fine." I wave him away, embarrassed by the blood-stained sheets. "I just—what are you doing?"

"I got this," he says easily, removing my soiled sheets. "Where can I find another set?"

I point to the linen closet in my bathroom. Derek shuffles into the bathroom and returns a moment later with fresh sheets.

I watch, dumbfounded, as he makes up my bed.

"You okay, Stellina? Hungry?" he asks as he tucks in the top sheet at the foot of my bed.

"What time is it?" I wonder.

"About ten p.m."

"Wow. I slept the whole day."

Derek shrugs as he fluffs my pillows. "You needed the rest."

"I guess. Have you been here all day?"

"Most of it," he says.

I frown. What the hell has he done all day? "Have you hung out with Levi?"

"I moved." He straightens, his work done.

"Moved?" I mutter. What is he talking about?

Derek smiles. "I'm your new roommate."

"Wh—what?" I sputter. "What about Levi? What do you mean—"

As I ask him questions, he exits my bedroom and returns with a duffle bag tossed over his shoulder. He plops it on the floor at the foot of my bed. Looks at me and grins.

"I get that you don't want to leave your brother. And that this is your space, and you're comfortable here. So, I came to you."

"What?" I repeat, trying to process what's happening. "You can't just—"

"I'm here, babe. Whatever you need, I got it. I meant every damn thing I said to you, Stellina. I'm not fucking running. But I can't be here, in LA, and not be with you either. So, I moved in."

I stare at him for several beats, my mouth dropping open in shock.

He laughs and pulls me into a hug. Drops a kiss to the top of my head.

"I know this is fucked. It's hard and it's way out of my comfort zone. But we'll figure this out. Together. Me and you. I got you, Allegra. Lean on me all you want, babe. I won't fucking crack."

I wrap my arms around his waist and press my ear against his chest. Listen to the rhythm of his heart.

I won't fucking crack.

For the first time in a long time, I believe him. Maybe it's because I feel like I'm cracking. Or splintering. Or maybe it's because we're both already a little chipped.

Whatever the reason, I don't protest Derek's announcement. Even though I don't fully trust him or his promise to stay. Even though I don't like him making decisions—like asking the doctor about my future fertility and moving himself into my home—without speaking to me about them first, I let it go.

Instead, I let him hold me. I let him ask me, again, if I'm hungry. I let him and Levi and the Clovers take care of me.

For the rest of the night, I stop worrying about things outside of my control and grieve my little fruit slice. When we crawl into bed later that night, Derek holds me in his arms. He breathes in the scent of my hair. His hands hold me together.

He kisses away the tears that stream down my cheeks.

The loss that ebbs and flows in my veins. The pain that twists my chest and gathers in my abdomen.

My baby is gone. My heart is broken.

He makes soothing sounds at the gasps that fall from my lips as my tears grow into sobs.

And he doesn't waver. Not even once.

Derek doesn't crack.

I do.

NINE
DEREK

HE STRAIGHTENS when he sees me. With his hands shoved into the pockets of his jeans, his hair styled in a trendy fashion, and his eyes—the same shade as mine—boring into me, there's no doubt in my mind that Dex is my biological father.

My gut confirms what the paternity test already proved.

He's got an edge to him, a swagger, that's innate. He's a little closed off, a touch aloof, maybe even unapproachable. I know that look; I wear it daily.

But where Dex is different, more mature I guess, is in his ability to drop the mask and grin. A real fucking smile, when he sees me.

"Glad you came," he tosses out, his tone casual. But I see the relief in his eyes. Knowing he wants to connect with me, that he didn't give up when I tossed up roadblock after speed bump, soothes something I didn't know I needed.

It allows me to relax. To drop my guard a bit. To fucking smile back. "Yeah."

"This place does a mean mushroom burger," Dex says, pulling open the door for me.

I snort. "I love mushrooms."

He grins. "Me too."

He doesn't tack on anything else. *Like father, like son.* Or one of those hokey bullshit lines. I like that about him.

I hang back as he talks to the hostess. We're led to a high-top table in the back of what appears to be a trendy, yet low-key, sports bar. It's clean and contemporary but with a chill vibe instead of the flashiness of LA.

I slide onto a barstool. We order a couple of Cokes.

"How's Allegra?" Dex asks. Poor bastard. He probably thinks she's a safe topic. An icebreaker.

I sigh. "She's not doing too great."

His eyes snap to mine. Pure concern in his gaze. Fuck, my chest squeezes. The fact that he cares for my girl, looks out for her, endears him to me more.

"She was pregnant," I continue, watching his expression for any sign of judgement.

There's none. Just compassion and worry. Fucking love. But who doesn't love my Stellina?

"It was...ours. Mine and hers." I clear my throat. "Ectopic," I spit out the word. Meet his eyes. "That's when—"

Dex dips his head. "Unviable."

"Yeah," I say, relieved I don't have to explain it. I hardly understand all the intricacies myself. "They gave her a shot to stop the growth and..." I shrug.

Dex nods. Meets my eyes again. "How are you holding up? Processing?"

Fuck. Something kicks behind my breast plate. The back of my nose burns and my tongue feels too thick, too big, for my fucking mouth. I've been so focused on my Stellina, so worried about her, that considering my own feelings seemed selfish.

Haven't I been selfish enough?

I clear my throat. Turn away and stare at a ball game playing out on TV.

Dex glances at a menu he doesn't need to read, giving me space to pull my shit together.

Our Cokes arrive and I grasp the cold glass. Dex orders two mushroom burgers, shooting me a quick glance. I nod my acceptance, grateful he's taking the lead here.

When our server is gone, I exhale. "It's a lot," I admit.

"I'll say," he agrees, gripping his drink. "I wish I could say it gets easier, but it doesn't."

I frown. "What do you mean?"

"When you love someone the way you obviously care for Allegra, it's for life. The worry, the concern, the caring, it gets bigger. Keeps growing. Even more so when you have a kid." He shrugs. "I'm sorry for your loss, Derek. Real fucking sorry."

"Thank you," I murmur. He's the first person to address my feelings on the issue. I lift my Coke higher, tip it toward him, and take a swig.

"You sticking around?" Again, there's no judgement in his tone. Is that part of being a parent? Showing up for your kid in whatever capacity they need and not judging them for the choices that got them into the mess they're in?

A bead of anger pulses through me as I think of Allegra's parents. Where the hell are they? How could they not show up when she's suffering like this?

Do they even know? Did Levi tell them?

I sigh, recalling an exchange I had with Mrs. Rousell many, many years ago.

I'll look out for him, I promised her.

Please, keep him safe. He's not prepared for the world the way you are. This is all he knows. She pointed to her small house on the hill.

He's made for more, I declared. *He deserves more.*

Her eyes were sad when they met mine. I didn't fully understand her look, but it was filled with heartache. Longing. *I'll pray for you.*

I fucking laughed. I didn't want anyone's prayers.

Maybe I should've thanked her.

Hell, I could use some fucking deity vibes.

And I could've used a parent a long time ago.

But now, you have Dex.

I shake the thought away. I barely know the man sitting across the table from me. And yet, something in his sharp gaze lets me know he's sticking around. Even if I don't.

But... "Yeah. I am. I'm here for her. Whatever she needs," I say.

The side of his mouth tugs up, the same way mine does when I'm trying not to smile. "Good."

I sip my Coke.

Dex heaves out a sigh. "I didn't know about you," he says out of nowhere.

Okay, we're doing this. I sit up straighter, hunch forward over the table.

"I only learned when your mother passed," he admits. "And then, I wasn't in the right shape to reach out to you. But, knowing about you, fuck, what a wakeup call. Thank you, Derek." He tips his glass toward me like a salute.

"For what?"

Dex smirks. "You got me clean. Sober. No way I would've taken that step without a relationship with you to hope for."

"You went to rehab?" I blurt out, my eyebrows knitting.

"Yep. Got sober, got out, changed my life. Made new fucking friends. And started Beirut."

"It's a successful club."

"It pays the bills." Great, he's modest too.

"And Allegra?" I ask.

"I had no fucking clue," Dex barks out a laugh. "I was knocked on my ass when I saw you with her. She'd been talking about an ex—"

"I was never just her ex," I clarify. She was always my North Star.

Dex grins. "But I had no idea it was you. This is LA, man. There's as many musicians as actors and lawyers."

"Yeah," I snort, seeing his point. "That's fair."

"After you bounced, she pulled back," he admits. "Came by for her last check and it was good to see that she was okay. That you guys were talking. She's one hell of a woman; I'm glad you're back."

"Me too," I agree. "I didn't know my mom died until... you know, you."

Dex frowns, his eyebrows knitting together. "No one told you?"

I shrug. "Must've been one of those cases that slipped through the cracks." I can't hide the bitterness in my tone and Dex catches it.

His eyes narrow. "I sense you were one of those cases a lot."

I nod. "Too many times."

"Fuck. I'm sorry. If I had known..."

"Yeah. You and my mom...was it, well, what was it?"

Dex sighs. "Judy was a beautiful and vivacious woman. So full of life. Smart and happy." He squints, as if he's conjuring an image of her in his mind. "It was a summer. Not even. It was a July that I could've lived in forever."

I hunch closer, drawn to his words. I wish I could step into this picture he's painting and live in it for a minute. "Where'd you meet?"

Dex grins. "We met on the Fourth of July. In Boston, near the waterfront. It was rough then, the South side. She was wearing an American flag as a tube top. She had long hair, blonde—your mother. And blue, blue eyes. Not like you, sorry, man." He points to his brown eyes. "These guys started messing with her and…"

"You stepped in," I supply.

He nods. "Ended up with a split lip."

"Really?"

"Yeah. Judy dragged me to an Irish pub to get some ice. We had a pint and…"

"It was a month," I conclude.

"One of the best of my life. But then, I had to get back to college. I was studying in Indiana. I was only supposed to be in Boston for the Fourth weekend, sleeping on my buddy's couch. I stayed, for her. But when August rolled around, she wouldn't see me. Said there was no point, since I was leaving, and she was staying. That we were a summer fling, and I had my whole future ahead of me. She never told me she was expecting. She never told me anything. I went down to the waterfront to see her, and she was there, flirting and laughing with the same guy who busted my lip. I was young and—"

"I would've been fucking furious," I interject, imagining if Allegra pulled that shit with me. Recalling the way I reacted at Taps over the summer, dragging her right off the damn bar.

"I was. I took off, went back to Indiana, and never heard from Judy again." Dex takes a gulp of his Coke.

Our mushroom burgers arrive, and our conversation

pauses as we thank the server and fix our plates. Salt, pepper, ketchup.

"I'm sorry," I tell him.

He glances up. "For what?"

"For all the years I spent resenting you. Fuck, I fucking hated that I had a dad who bailed. Mom was good in the early years but once she started messing with drugs, I ended up in foster care. And that was..."

Dex's grip on the edge of the tabletop tightens. Hard.

"It was hell," I admit. "And I hated you for leaving me in that situation."

"I'm sorry," he whispers, the blood draining from his face. I know he's imagining countless horrors. I don't say anything to ease his mind because my experiences, as a kid, were fucking horrors. The things nightmares are made from.

But... "I got through it. Made some solid friendships. Formed the band. I'm resilient, Dex. Guess I get that from you."

He nods slightly. "I wish I gave you a lot more than that, Derek."

I stare at him for a long moment. Watch as he picks up his burger, takes a bite, chews thoughtfully.

Do I still want a dad? Could this mean something real? Something more than a common courtesy, let's meet and clear the air?

I think of everything Allegra told me about this man. My father.

I release an exhale. "You still can," I tell him.

His eyes snap to mine. They're dark and glinting. But in the center, right around his pupils, hope flares.

Fucking hope. It'll kill you every damn time.

"I'd like that," he says, not making it more than what it is. An olive branch.

"Me too," I quip, before picking up my burger.

We eat in silence for a few moments. Dex navigates our conversation to lighter topics. Now that the heaviness of the first meeting is out of the way, we talk music. Sports. Life in LA.

I tell him about River Wells. He asks if I want to distribute to Beirut.

He tells me about the years he spent in the Middle East and the woman he fell in love with in Lebanon, the reason why he named his club after a city once deemed the "Paris of the Middle East."

We laugh. Rattle off a few jokes. Fucking bond.

He picks up the tab and I let him. When he extends a hand, I shake it firmly. We agree to meet the following week, for more burgers.

And as I drive back to Allegra's place, I realize I can't wait to see her. To tell her about my meeting with Dex. To talk to her about the father I'm getting a chance to know.

Even as the sorrow of our loss hangs low in my gut, the hope in my chest swells larger.

That fucking hope that just won't quit.

I'm gutted that Allegra and I lost a baby. But I also know there's a future for us. I hope it's one with children.

Given her upbringing, does she want kids? Would she want to try again? When she thinks of her future, what does she see?

For me, it's so clear now. Fucking obvious, like a neon sign.

I want her. I want to create the family I never had.

The one I'm still fucking hoping for.

TEN

ALLEGRA

"HOW'D IT GO?" I ask over my shoulder when he comes through the front door.

Derek pauses in the foyer, freezes like the image of me pulls him up short. I glance down at the matching pajama set Nova sent me. I turn away to continue stirring the honey in my tea.

When I don't hear his approach, I glance back at him. "What's wrong?"

A slow smile rolls over Derek's face. He shakes his head once, as if to clear it, as if to tell me absolutely nothing is wrong when every fucking thing sure isn't right. But at the sight of his boyish, flippant gesture, my body relaxes.

Derek walks over and wraps his arms around me from behind, his hands clasping right below my belly button.

Fruit slice. I try not to wince.

Derek nuzzles his cheek against mine and presses a kiss to my shoulder.

"It went well?" I inquire, my body further relaxing at his sweetness. It must have gone well for Derek to be at ease. I melt into his frame and pull in a cleansing breath. Maybe things are changing for the better. Maybe this cautious optimism is the first step forward.

He heaves out an exhale. "Better than I thought."

I turn in his arms to see his face. "And?"

His eyes hold mine. He grins. "He, Dex, he's a good guy."

"He is," I agree.

"Told me about my mom," he tacks on.

I gesture toward the table and Derek pulls out a chair for me. Once I'm seated, he moves toward the kitchen and pours a mug of tea for himself while the kettle is still hot. We sit together, sipping our teas, our eyes meeting and holding.

And it feels familiar. Easy. Even given the recent distance between us.

"He really didn't know about me," Derek admits.

"Yeah," I breathe out softly.

"Fuck," he chuckles. Turning away, he grips the back of his neck. When he meets my eyes again, his are filled with a maturity, a wisdom, that wasn't there a few weeks ago. "It's hard to be angry with a guy who didn't know you existed. He tried to do right by my mom but she…" Derek trails off. Clears his throat. "She pushed him away. And the way he tells it, it's as if she didn't want to tie him down. It's as if she looked at him and knew, this guy could do something real, something that matters. She cut him loose not to hold him back and then…" He bites his bottom lip. Emotion swells in his eyes and he blinks faster. I reach across the table to place my hand on his. "And then she cost me a father. Fuck, Stellina, it's hard to be angry with a dead woman too."

"Derek," I murmur. Sliding from my chair, I round the table and move to sit on the chair beside his.

But he doesn't let me. Instead, his arms dart out. They wrap around my waist and pull me into his frame. I sit on his lap as he wraps me in his arms. I drape my arms around his neck, hold his cheek to my chest.

His grip is relentless. His pain is tangible, scenting the air with despair and regret. I squeeze him tighter. This time, it's me, holding the pieces of him as he cracks. Breaks. Accepts what is and what will never be.

"I'm sorry," I tell him.

"I am too," he admits. Clearing his throat again, he peers back up at me. "That's the worst fucking part. I'm sorry. Sorry about the wasted fucking years. Sorry my mom couldn't hold it together the way she probably thought she would. Sorry Dex lived half his life never knowing he had a kid. Sorry I missed out on all those years with both of them. And so fucking sorry, goddamn remorseful, Allegra, that I couldn't be the man you needed when you needed *me*. I sound like a broken record. How many times am I going to apologize to you? How many times am I going to fucking fail?"

"Derek." I place a palm on his cheek. "Listen to me. You didn't leave me, you left—"

"Because I couldn't handle the truth. I couldn't process it," he cuts me off.

"It was a lot to process," I say gently.

He shakes his head. "But you deserve a guy that can handle it. The one that won't fucking crack."

"Sometimes we need to crack so we can heal even stronger. Become resilient. Being weathered isn't the same as being broken."

"I love you, Allegra," he says the words resolutely. Like a thunderclap. A proclamation. "I love you so fucking much. And I don't know what you want, or what you envision, or any of it. But I want you. I want your future. I want to marry you one day and put my babies in your belly." His hand grips my abdomen protectively. "I want to grow a fucking family unlike the ones we came from. A family that's all about the love and the moments. I want it all with you, my little star. And it makes me so fucking hopeful, more excited than terrified. That's how I know it's true. I know it in my bones. It's me and you."

I blink at him.

Holy shit.

I wasn't expecting that. The declaration, the promise, the *knowing*.

"I need you to mean it," I whisper, too scared to fall again. To give my heart and my head over to what he's offering.

"I'll prove it to you. I promise." His eyes bleed with sincerity. Certainty.

And something inside me shifts. I've known a part of Derek he doesn't show the world since the night of my seventeenth birthday.

None of those girls hold a candle to a little star like you.

He saw me when I was invisible. He kissed me that night but the confidence he slipped into my mouth took root and blossomed. He gave me a gift and I never forgot it.

With his dark eyes pouring apologies and hopes, dreams and wants, into mine, I kiss him.

It's a press of lips at first. Sweet and sincere. Tender and heartfelt. But when he parts his lips, my tongue slips inside and I *kiss* him.

Years ago, Derek changed my world with a simple first kiss.

Today, I promise him a future with a different type of exchange.

Our lips move over each other's slowly. Our tongues meet and dance, touch and taste.

I slip him forgiveness and he sips my sorrow. I share the grief lining my bones and he steps into its shadow, beside me. My lips flutter hope over his and his fingers hold my frame with the stability I've yearned for.

Our kiss turns hungry, and I shift in his lap. Practically straddling him, I moan lightly as he stiffens beneath me. My fingers toy with the hair at the back of his head. His hold on me tightens. He drags his mouth away from my lips and kisses down the column of my neck. I arch into him.

I want this. Everything he promised me. The future, the ring on my finger, and the babies in my belly.

Yes, it's too soon. Of course, the timing is all wrong.

But I can see it. With the same clarity of his words, I can imagine his heart's desires.

Because I want it—*him*—too. I always have.

"Derek," I murmur.

"Hmm?" he asks before he pushes to his feet, swinging me in his arms. He carries me to my bedroom and places me in the center of the bed.

Sitting beside me, he brushes my hair from my face. "You need rest, beauty."

"I'm okay," I tell him.

"I know you are. You're strong and brave and fucking resilient. But you need rest. And I need your forgiveness."

I frown. "You have it." I point toward the kitchen. "I gave it to you."

He smirks. "I haven't earned it yet, though. And I need to do that. For me as much as for you." He moves closer to me and wraps an arm around my shoulders.

We lie down together, turning our bodies to face each other. Derek kisses the tip of my nose.

"It's too soon," he whispers.

I sigh. Logically, I know he's right. I need to wait weeks to have sex. Knowing that doesn't make me want him any less, especially once we start kissing. "Part of me wants you to fill me up so I don't feel so empty," I admit.

Heartache explodes in his eyes. He laces his fingers with mine. "You're not empty, Stellina. You're aching."

"Yeah," I admit, snuggling closer to him. "I didn't even want a baby. I know I wasn't ready. But when I saw that positive pregnancy test, everything changed. And I believed in it, the future, the family, my little piece of fruit, like it was real."

"It was. It is," Derek presses.

I sigh heavily. "I want children one day. A family. Like the one you spoke about."

He kisses me again. "Sleep, my love. We're together. We're okay."

"I love you, Derek," I whisper. "Even when I don't want to. Even when it's hard. I love you." My eyelids grow heavy.

I feel his smile against my lips. "Always, Allegra."

I close my eyes, let the pull of sleep take me.

I dream of the garden. It's colorful again, although more muted than the first time I wandered through its flower beds.

But there's color. There are birds and flowers and the soothing sounds of rustling branches.

It relieves my hurt, restores my strength, and erases some of the ache.

I sit beneath a shady oak tree and close my eyes.

And in the gentle breeze that passes, I feel it.

Acceptance.

Understanding.

Trust.

I breathe it in deeply, hold it in my lungs, store it in my soul.

Trust in the future. Trust in family.

Trust in my little slice of fruit, a piece of heaven.

ELEVEN

DEREK

"THIS IS where you're recording the new album?" Allegra asks, stepping deeper into Hendrix's studio.

I splay an arm out. "This is it."

"Chill space."

"Henny's a chill guy," I admit. Pointing to the hallway, I add, "He lives in the apartment overhead. Don't be surprised if he pops down."

Allegra nods. Glancing around the empty booth, she asks, "Where is everyone?"

I smirk. "They're coming. I wanted to play something for you first."

Her eyes light up. She tucks her hair, brunette and wavy and finally growing, behind her ears. "My song?"

"Stellina's song," I agree, hoping she likes it.

I bring her into the booth with me and sit her on a chair. Nerves buzz along my palms, half in anticipation, half in fear.

I'm laying it all out for her. But I need her to know the depth of my feelings. The intensity of my heartache over almost losing her. Again. The power in the love that I feel for her, even when I don't know how to show it.

It's been a week since I told her how much I want her, our future, our family. Seven nights of sleeping beside her, listening to the even sounds of her breathing. Eight mornings of pouring her coffee, taking her to the hospital to check her HCG levels, and reminding her to rest.

A whole week of listening to Levi jokingly bitch about me coming out of his sister's bedroom. Even though we're boys again, brothers, there's an edge there. A new line that we both know better than to cross. In some ways, he needs to let me take the lead with Allegra. In others, I need to accept that he's always going to be an important man in her life.

It's been a period of adjustment. Transition. Growth.

And now, I'm taking the next step forward.

I settle myself on a barstool and fiddle with my guitar. Glance at my girl. My fucking beauty. "You ready?"

Her hands are folded in her lap. Her ankles crossed. She's such a fucking good girl; I still can't believe she's mine.

"Ready," she confirms.

I pull in an inhale, steel my nerves, and strum out the opening notes of my song.

Her song.

Then, I sing it to her. I don't hold back. I close my eyes and let the music, parts of my soul, surge forth like a tidal wave and scoop us both up in its powerful current.

You vanished like daybreak,
Lost stars and forgotten night.
You haunt me like a shadow,
Clingy and relentless.
You haunt me like her.

· · ·

ALLEGRA'S EYES are on mine, unblinking. Her expression is a cross between thoughtful and reminiscent. I glance down at my fingers, strumming my guitar, and start the second verse.

You faded like a photograph,
Broken memories and echoes of lost dreams,
You stalk me like my conscience,
Vile and futile,
You stalk me like pieces of her.

UNDERSTANDING COLORS HER EXPRESSION. Her eyes close for a beat, sadness and defeat in her expression. When her eyes open, they hold mine, pinning me to the moment. What a beautiful fucking moment.

Stars die and places merge,
You turned my rebellion into a
Resentment that burns.
All-consuming and exhausting,
You hate me like her.
No, you hate me like me.

HEARTBREAK PIERCES HER IRISES. Tears well in her eyes. One slips down her cheek, rolling in slow motion, as I track it with my gaze. *Don't fucking cry, Stellina.* The words don't come, because the next verse is starting. This time, my voice is deeper. The rawness seeps out, the hurt wraps around the words, and I sing them with every cell in my being.

Vanished day and faded moments,
Broken memories and lost dreams,
Stars burn too bright before they extinguish,

And baby, I'm blazing for you.
Yeah, you hate me like me.
Girl, I fucking love you like you.

I LOVE *you more than the stars,*
    In spite of the loss,
    Beyond the destruction.
    You glow; I sear,
    Together, we're too bright
    To smother.
    So I'll suffocate on our hurt,
    And wrap you in my love,
    Because, Stellina, it's always been you.

WHEN I FINISH, Allegra is openly crying. Before I can slide from my barstool or lower my guitar, she's rushing me. I swing my guitar to the side to catch my girl as she vaults into my arms.

Allegra sobs into the crook of my neck, her hands fisting the material of my T-shirt, her breath hot as it traps between my skin and shirt.

"Shh, baby, don't cry," I soothe, my hands splay across her back.

"That was beautiful, Derek," she tells me.

"You're beautiful," I remind her.

"And heartbreaking."

"My heart's a little banged up," I admit.

"I'm sorry about your mom," she confesses.

"I'm sorry about us."

Allegra sighs. Pulling back, she wipes her eyes and

shakes her head. "Don't be. We're right where we're supposed to be. It's me and you."

I take her hand and tug her closer. I hate when there's space between us. It's fucked up because I used to crave it. Need it to function.

Now, I can't think when she's not nearby.

"Always me and you," I promise.

Allegra smiles. It's soft and sweet and so damn sunny it hurts to look at.

How can a woman who has lost as much as her sob so beautifully? How can a woman as strong as her wear her vulnerability like a shield of armor?

"I love you, Derek," she tells me, kissing me hard.

"Always you, baby." I grip the back of her head and deepen our kiss, slanting my mouth over hers and sneaking my tongue inside.

I feel her smile before her hands find purchase on my shoulders. She steps between my parted thighs. My hands grip the backs of hers, right below the swell of her delectable ass cheeks.

We stay like that, making out in the middle of the booth. Like fucking horny teenagers. Or star-crossed lovers. Like two people trying to figure out what's what. Two adults yearning for a future that's brighter than their combined pasts.

In this moment, we're everything. All the moments that led to this one. All the broken pieces and hurtful exchanges, all the touches and kisses and lovemaking on rainy days and in open sunshine.

We come together and it's so fucking right; it's permanent.

The clearing of a throat, loud, obnoxious, and annoying, jars me from my slice of peace.

I pull away angrily, my eyes swinging to the door.

I swear when I see him standing there. "You're ruining my moment, Henny."

Hendrix laughs. It's a big, hearty, unconcerned rumble. He steps closer to us. "You sure? I've been here for a minute."

Allegra ducks her head, embarrassed. She bites her bottom lip, color flooding her cheeks. Damn, she's beautiful.

"You must be Allegra," Hendrix says, holding out a hand. "I'm Hendrix. Heard a lot about you."

"It's good to meet you." Allegra shakes his hand. "I'm, uh, sorry we—"

"Don't be," Hendrix interrupts. "The music sounds better when real life happens to it."

Allegra grins.

"The boys are gonna be here in five. You ready to record?" Hendrix asks me.

I glance at Allegra. Squeeze her hand. "Yeah, I'm ready."

Hendrix nods. "All right. I'll get some things set up for you." He glances at Allegra. "I take it I'll be seeing you around?"

"You will," I answer for her.

"I'll be here," she confirms.

Hendrix chuckles. "Glad to hear it. Make yourself at home. The coffee's over there." He points to another door.

"Thanks, Hendrix," Allegra says. "I'm going to grab a cup before you guys begin."

"All right." I tap her ass lightly and watch as she exits the booth and enters the small kitchen with a coffee machine.

"All good?" Hendrix asks.

"Better than good," I admit without looking at him.

"Keep it that way," he warns.

"I will." This time, I know it's the truth. I'm all in, forever.

The boys arrive a few minutes later.

I hold back and watch as they embrace Allegra.

Levi kisses the top of her head. Jameson gives her a big bear hug. Mav says something that makes her laugh.

She has no idea how much she means to all of us. As individuals and as a group. She's a Clover now, one of us.

And a band like ours, with our history, our complicated screw-ups, our friendship, it's forever. It's a found family that rivals even the best of real families.

We're all in it for always.

Just like my Stellina and me.

She takes a seat as we begin to warm up. She watches intently as we mess around with a few songs and get into the headspace of recording an album.

Over the next two weeks, we come together. We bicker. We try new things. We argue. We make great fucking music. The kind that makes you dig into your gut, pull out your pain, and lay it out for everyone to dissect. The type that heals parts of your soul.

Through it all, Allegra is there.

Studying for her final exams just outside the booth. Reading a book. Watching us curiously. Weighing in with opinions when we ask. Judging our disagreements even when we tell her to stay out of it.

She centers us in a way we're not used to. She gives us the stability we used to topple over. She heals some of our cracks with her patience, and in turn, we give her our strength.

At the end of two weeks, The Burnt Clovers has a completed album.

The band has a restored sweetheart.

And Allegra and me are back in a real, true, forever kind of relationship.

It's all love and moments.

Pure magic.

TWELVE
ALLEGRA

I FEEL STRONGER with each day that passes. Physically, emotionally, spiritually. With Derek by my side, with Levi's presence, with Mav's jokes and Jameson's dependability, my grief ebbs.

Plus, I've got my girls. They bundle me in support, lend me their ears, and show up whenever I need them.

"What are we drinking?" Nova asks as she collapses on my couch.

Kenny rolls her eyes. "We can't drink. We're in the middle of final exams."

Ivy and I exchange a look before we burst out laughing.

Mckenna huffs, Ivy uncorks a bottle of red wine, and I shrug. "Finals are almost over," I tell Mckenna.

"This is bad karma," she disagrees, gesturing toward the wine glasses Nova passes out. "Celebrating before we passed. One of us could fail and—"

"It won't be you, so don't worry," Nova assures her.

Ivy snickers and lifts her glass. "To final exams."

The four of us dissolve into giggles before clinking glasses and sipping our wine.

"How are things going?" Ivy asks as she leans back in Levi's favorite chair.

I smile. "Good. The band is wrapping up their album."

Nova rolls her eyes. "I'm happy for them, but really, I want to know what's up with you and Derek. Baby Daddy Reign is giving off major commitment vibes."

Mckenna winces.

"What?" Nova asks.

Baby Daddy, Kenny mouths.

"Too soon," Ivy agrees.

Regret blossoms on Nova's face as her eyes meet mine. "A, I'm so sorry. I didn't mean—"

"No," I cut her off. "Honestly, your humor is refreshing. And, one day, Derek will be the hottest baby daddy of all time."

Nova laughs nervously. "He will," she agrees.

"Things are going...great," I admit. "Derek's different. More stable, settled, honest. He's still speaking with his therapist, Kris, via Zoom, and I see him working on things. Working through things." I shrug. "We're in a good place."

Ivy grins. "I'm happy for you, Allegra."

"Yeah," Kenny echoes. "You deserve this. And I see him trying too. It's obvious that he loves you more than anything else in his world."

"Totally," Nova agrees. She glances around the condo. "Where is he, anyway? It's rare for Derek not to be loitering around you."

Ivy snorts. "I bribed Levi to keep him out for at least two hours so we could talk about them."

We look at each other and laugh again.

"Wait! What'd you bribe Levi with?" Nova demands, waggling her eyebrows.

Ivy blows her a kiss. "I never kiss and tell."

"Oh, God," Kenny groans, assuming the worst.

Knowing that Ivy is joking, I snort in laughter. Glancing at my friends, I'm grateful to have them. Even during this period of grief and sorrow, I know I'm loved. I know I have true friends who care about me and will always show up, no matter what.

Instead of watching a movie, we drink wine, order take-out, and gossip about the men in our lives until two of them stride into the condo. Derek is at the lead, and he pulls me against his frame and kisses me.

"You have a final exam tomorrow," he reminds me.

I roll my eyes.

Levi smirks. "Since when did you become a stickler for the rules?" he asks Derek.

Derek ignores him and tosses me over his shoulder.

As he strides toward my bedroom, the girls cheer and whistle.

"Good night, ladies," Derek says. "Go home and study."

Baby Daddy Reign, Nova mouths at me.

Again, I erupt in laughter. It feels good to smile again.

SLOWLY, while the band makes an album and my friends rally around, I put myself back together. I find myself again. I'm able to think of my little fruit slice and be grateful for the miracle of what was instead of drowned with the sorrow of what is.

I'm able to thank him or her for bringing their daddy back into my life. This time, I know Derek is unshakeable. He won't crack. And now, neither will I.

For two weeks, I sit in the recording studio and study for

exams. Read poetry books. And listen to music that fills up my emptiness.

When Derek and I step out of Hendrix's studio after the album wraps, we're hand in hand, grinning from ear to ear.

"Wanna do something wild?" he asks.

"Don't you want to celebrate with the guys?"

Derek shakes his head. "Not when I could be with you."

"What do you have in mind?" I bite my bottom lip.

While Derek and I are back together, we haven't really gone out. I've been processing and taking final exams; he's been recording. Instead of dinner dates and days at the beach, we've been adjusting to our new normal.

Trusting each other.

"Come on." He tugs me closer to his parked Camry.

"Hey!" my brother shouts. "Where're you going?"

"Got plans!" Derek raises our joined hands in the air. He grins at my brother. "Don't wait up for us."

Levi swears but he's grinning. I blow him a kiss and he waves back.

Derek and I slide into his car and he pulls onto the street, leaving the studio behind as he turns onto the highway.

We stop for a snack and coffees before resuming our drive.

"Where are we going?" I wonder.

Derek reaches over to tap my thigh. "You'll see." He grins and for a blink, he looks more like a boy than a rock god.

I relax in my seat, liking the weight of his hand on my leg.

"Tired?" he wonders.

I yawn in response. "A little. But I'll catch up on sleep now that finals are finished."

"Close your eyes, beauty. We've got a bit of a ride."

I glance at him. I really am tired. "You sure?"

"Absolutely."

I nod once, letting my eyes close. The movement of the car, coupled with the music streaming through the speakers, lulls me to sleep.

I wake when the car stops.

"Stellina." Derek's voice is gentle. "Wake up, baby. We're here."

I force my eyes open and glance around groggily. "Where?"

Derek's smile comes into my line of sight.

Behind him, I see the signs. And I laugh. Oh, I bend over and crack up. "You brought me to Disneyland?"

"Yep," he quips. "Come on. Mickey's waiting."

"You mean Minnie," I correct him, clearing the sleep from my eyes. I check my reflection in the overhead mirror. My hair is a mess and I have a crease on the side of my face from the seat belt, but my eyes are clear. My expression open.

I look happier than I have in weeks.

Slipping from the car, I meet Derek at the front. He clasps my hand and moves us toward the entrance.

"Let's have some fun, Allegra. God knows we earned it."

I move closer to him, snuggling into his side when he wraps his arm around my waist.

"Let's do it," I agree.

We're stopped four times on our way to the entrance by fans wanting Derek's autograph. He stops, signs their gear, and exchanges polite conversation.

But the fifth time we're stopped, he grins sheepishly. He swipes his signature over a starter cap and points to me. "See that woman?"

"Yeah?" the kid wonders.

"I'm trying to woo her," he explains.

"What's a woo?" the kid wonders.

The boy's mother's expression softens. She takes her son's hand. "Thanks for the autograph." She glances at me. "Hope he wins at the wooing."

I laugh. "Yeah, me too."

The woman smiles and whisks her son away.

Derek returns to my side. "I haven't won already?"

I laugh and bite my bottom lip, pretending to consider.

He smacks my ass as we resume walking to the entrance. "Today, I'm pulling out all my best moves," he warns.

"I can't wait to see them."

Derek chuckles. "Yeah, me too. Since you're the first woman I've ever tried to woo."

"I'm already in love with you," I let him off the hook.

"All the more reason to prove myself," he counters.

I smile. He grins. And together, we enter the most magical place on Earth.

Disneyland.

AFTER SPACE MOUNTAIN, Big Thunder Railroad, and the Star Wars: Rise of the Resistance rides, Derek and I settle into a little boat for a turnaround "it's a small world."

As we move through the singing dolls, I glance over at Derek. "I like today."

"Me too, Stellina."

"Want to meet Minnie next?" I ask.

He nods. "And get a pretzel."

"Or popcorn," I tack on.

"We'll eat dinner," he promises.

We finish the ride and wait in line to meet Minnie. Mickey comes over during our photo op and the characters make a big deal of meeting Derek. It's hilarious and entertaining. He charms them both as well as the kids (and their parents) waiting in line.

One mom convinces him to sing.

Derek shakes his head but acquiesces, getting down on one knee to serenade me.

Cameras flash and a few women sigh audibly. Kids rush him and he spends thirty minutes signing autographs, shooting me an apologetic look. But since it's kids, I know he can't say no. And I respect him for it.

Instead, I hang back and let him do his thing.

When he's done, he wraps an arm around my shoulders. "I owe you all the ice cream and popcorn and pretzels."

I laugh. "Dinner is fine."

He chuckles and kisses me right on the lips. "I love you, little star."

"I love you too, Derek."

He takes me to dinner at Blue Bayou. We sit for a long time, drinking wine and talking. In a way, it's the first date of our newest chapter.

The one where we've experienced a loss and somehow, with all the uncertainty, all the wariness, and pain, made it out the other side.

We made it to Disneyland. We embraced magic.

Love and moments.

"You want to live out here?" he asks randomly. "In California."

I shrug, glancing at him. "I don't know yet."

"Would you go back to Boston?" he presses, as if asking himself.

I shake my head. "I'm kind of waiting to see what pans out job wise. I didn't get the NGO position. They hired someone from their New York office who is moving out this way." I shrug. "I reached out to Vivi Yaeger at the Harrison Foundation. They have an office out here, as well as in Boston. But...yeah, I like it here. I like the weather. The vibe. My friends are all here so..."

"So, you'd want to stay?" He glances at me.

"Why are you asking?"

He smirks. "Curious, I guess."

"I think so. LA's been good to me. I feel like I grew up out here, you know?"

"Yeah," he murmurs. "I know."

"You ready to get going?" I ask as I polish off my wine.

"Sure, Stellina." Derek stands and reaches for my hand. He tosses a bunch of bills on the table, leaving a generous tip.

We walk slowly through the park, stopping a few times to snap a photo or for Derek to sign an autograph. When we make it back to the Camry, he points the car toward home.

I glance at him, wondering if he wants to stay out here too. Is Boston his home? Or the band? Or, one day, could it be me?

When we make it home, Levi and Mav are playing video games in the living room.

"Where's Jameson?" I wonder.

Levi tips his head toward the closed bedroom door. "On the phone."

"Amelia," Mav tacks on, making a scared face.

I chuckle. "Trouble in paradise?"

"Is it paradise when there's always trouble?" Mav wonders.

"Touché," Derek comments, dropping into a chair.

"What are you guys going to do now that the album's wrapped?" I ask, glancing at the three of them.

Mav smirks. "What are you going to do now that finals are finished?"

I laugh. "Good question."

"Fair question," Levi corrects, pressing pause on the game. He looks at me. "You want to stick around here?"

I glance between my brother and Derek. It's as if I just had this conversation over dinner. But Derek isn't exchanging a knowing glance with his best friend. Instead, his eyes are trained on me, his expression serious. His eyes curious.

My smile slips. "I don't know yet. I'm figuring things out."

"No job offers?" Mav asks, his statement devoid of judgement or sympathy.

"Not yet," I murmur.

Mav shrugs. "Take the summer and chill. You don't have to figure everything out overnight."

"Thanks, Mav," I say, relieved that someone gets it.

"So, we're cool to stay in town longer," Levi tacks on, confirming that I want to stay.

I nod. "I'm in." Maybe he's just asking to gauge if he should stick around in LA too?

"Great," my brother replies, unpausing the game.

As Levi and Mav return their attention to the video game, I relax. They're curious about my plans but not applying pressure on me to have my future mapped out.

When I look at Derek though, I sense the wheels turning in his mind.

"Will you keep working at the NGO?" Derek asks softly. "Through the summer? Or until a permanent gig comes up?"

"Yeah," I say. "That's kind of my plan for now." I drop into the corner of the couch.

"Are a lot of the staff around in the summer? Or do things quiet down?" he wonders.

I frown. "Some of the programs scale back but office operations, the overall mission, is all-year. Why?"

Derek shrugs but his gaze is sharp. "I bet more groups of people hang in that park at night during the summer..."

"I guess so."

"Maybe you could work mornings instead of evenings."

I shrug. "Maybe. But I like my schedule the way it is."

"Yeah, but your schedule is the way it is because you had class. Now that the semester is over, you could free up your nights. Not be leaving work when dusk is kicking up."

I narrow my eyes, trying to follow his line of thinking. "Are you worried?" I ask.

He sighs. "Of course, I'm worried, Allegra. That's not the best area and at nighttime—"

"I like the work I'm doing and I'm more than capable of taking care of myself," I cut him off.

He holds up his hands, palms out. As if he's a peace-keeper and I'm the hostile party in this conversation. "I'm just saying, maybe it's best to rethink—"

"It's not," I shoot him down again. "I like my schedule, and my life, the way it is. Right now."

He heaves out an exhale. "Fine."

"Fine," I reply, standing. "I'm going to sleep."

Derek drops his head back, as if I'm being irrational.

"More trouble in non-paradise," Mav mutters quietly.

My brother snorts.

"Good night," I say to the room.

"Night, A," Levi replies.

I glare at Derek.

"I'll be in in a bit," he says.

"I meant you too," I tell him. His eyes narrow. "About liking my life, the way it is right now. That includes me and you."

His expression softens and he nods. "I know, Stellina. Go get some rest."

I turn on my heel and move toward my bedroom. Once the door is closed, I change into my pajamas and slip into bed.

Today was fun. It was exciting and carefree.

Why do I need to have the rest of my life planned out just because I'm graduating next weekend? Why do I need to have a job lined up and a city chosen when the summer stretches before me, filled with possibilities?

I don't.

Satisfied with the decision of not making any big decisions, I close my eyes and fall asleep.

THIRTEEN
DEREK

AS ALLEGRA GATHERS with her friends for graduation activities, I find myself with time on my hands. The album has been recorded. The music that poured out of me during those weeks of self-reflection has tapered off. My need to create has subsided.

Allegra and I are in a good place. Our days are filled with a quiet familiarity I enjoy. We drink coffee together in the morning. I pick her up from the NGO in the evening. We eat dinner, sometimes the two of us, sometimes with the Clovers or her girls.

A routine emerges. A pattern. A comfortableness I'm unaccustomed to but now wonder how I lived so long without it. I feel like I'm finally home.

Home.

It's a strange concept. To me, it was always a word. The place where I crashed at the end of the day. Now, it's Allegra. It's her world, her dreams. My connection to her which causes me to view every aspect of my life through a new lens.

I kick at a rock as I walk down the street to meet Dex for

a burger. It's become our thing. Another part of my new normal that required adjustment. And yet, I'm not running from it. I'm staying, having the hard conversations, asking the questions.

Listening.

My therapist Kris reminds me to actively listen instead of hearing and waiting to speak. It's something I never thought about before yet made an impression on me. I think about the disagreements the band has had over the years. About Levi spiraling and checking into rehab. About Mav's desire to write more music.

I think about Allegra.

Fuck, it's hard growing up. Even harder to stay and learn. To fucking listen.

"How's it going?" Dex calls out when I approach the sports bar. Our spot.

Another puzzle piece to my new life.

I smile. "Pretty good."

"Pretty lost in thought," he calls me out.

I chuckle and shake his hand hello. We enter the bar, post up at our usual table, and exchange pleasantries with the server. After we order burgers and Cokes, Dex arches an eyebrow.

"All okay? Allegra?" he asks.

"She's good. She graduates on Saturday so..." I shrug.

"She's spending as much time with her friends before their lives head in different directions and you're wondering what the hell comes next," he surmises.

I glance up, surprised. "Is that a dad thing?"

Dex laughs, the wrinkles by his eyes crinkling. Except he doesn't look old. Weathered and wise in a way that makes me seek out his counsel. When did his opinion start to matter? When did Dex start to become my confidante as much as, maybe even more than, Kris?

"I don't know. Could be an old man thing," he replies, reading my thoughts again. "What's on your mind, Derek?"

I sigh and tap my fingers against the saltshaker. "Allegra's thinking of staying here. In LA."

Dex nods, as if he already knew this. Maybe he did. "You want to go back to Boston?"

I shrug. "The brownstone is always there. I want to be where my girl is."

Dex frowns. "So, stay."

Our server drops off our Cokes. We clink them together and take a pull.

"Yeah," I agree, nodding. "I think I should buy us a house."

Dex sputters, choking on his drink. He pounds against his chest, his dark brown eyes colliding with mine.

I grin. "Finally caught you off guard."

He coughs, clearing his throat. "You did that when I first realized who the hell you are."

I chuckle and he grins.

"You talk to her about it? Buying a house."

I shrug. "Not really. But I can't live in her room at Levi's forever. And my condo is a place I bought back in the day. Before we were together. A house, a place she can decorate however she wants, would be ours. You know?"

"I do." Dex nods, considering my words. "Still, I think you need to have this discussion with Allegra. Make sure she's on the same page as you."

"Yeah," I say. But who wouldn't want to be surprised with a house in LA? I know she likes it here. Her brother's local. Kenny is planning to attend law school, but Nova and

Ivy are sticking around. We could make this our home. Together.

"What else is going on?" Dex asks.

"Finished the album." I tell him all about our next album. About the song I wrote for Allegra. About the Clovers and the music and the way we're all clicking again.

And he listens. Dex, my dad, sits there and actively listens. It's one of the best afternoons of my life because it's so fucking simple. But real and meaningful and important.

Kris was right. Listening matters.

"I THINK WE SHOULD BUY A HOUSE," I announce that evening.

Allegra's eyes widen as they meet mine. "A house?"

"Yeah." I lean closer over the table between us.

We're at a sushi restaurant for dinner and right now, I want to swipe away all the plates so I can be closer to my girl. Read her expressions. Note the flecks of sage in her irises.

She frowns, her eyebrows pinching together.

"You don't want to live together?" I ask, pausing. My stomach hollows out and a coldness sweeps my limbs. Am I reading this wrong?

Is she not all in, the way I am?

Did losing the baby change something?

Is she not ready?

My thoughts spiral, rapid and tangled.

Allegra licks her bottom lip, her eyes bouncing between mine. "Derek, I, I don't know what comes next," she says softly. "I mean, I don't know where I'll get a permanent job offer. Or what will happen after the summer. Or…"

"Or what?" I murmur.

She shakes her head. "I feel like I just told you a few nights ago that I like things the way they are. Right now. Me and you, included."

"You did," I agree.

She frowns. "Besides, aren't we already living together?"

"In Levi's place." Bitterness coats my words.

"In my place too," she corrects me. Smiles hesitantly. "You and me, this, sometimes it's like a tornado."

Even though she says it lightly, her meaning is clear. Tornados bring destruction. My expression falls.

She sees it because she sighs. "I didn't mean it the way you're thinking."

"How'd you mean it?" I ask, my voice tight. I'm overreacting. Of course, I am. Allegra's had an intense few weeks but...fuck, I hate not knowing what she's thinking.

I hate how needy I feel. How badly I want her reassurances. I fucking need her to tell me it's going to be okay. It's going to work out. We're going to work out.

Shit. Is this how I've made her feel? Over and over and over again?

I groan. "I deserve this hell."

She snorts. "This isn't hell." She reaches across the table and takes my wrist. Gives it a little shake. "Derek, we've been going at max speed. I mean, it's been...a lot. Even you can admit that?"

I nod. I can admit it.

"I need to...think. Process. Take a beat. I like where we're at right now. This is enough for me. You know that."

I heave out a sigh. Nod again. "Okay," I say. "I get it."

And I do. But...I still want more. I want her fucking

future. My ring on her finger. Babies and moments and magic.

I want all her fucking sunshine, so I never have to stick to the shadows again.

"Okay," she agrees, giving me a little smile. "Let's enjoy our dinner. This date. This weekend, I graduate. Next weekend, the girls and I are coming to the Clovers show. We'll pregame and hang out and cheer for you guys. Maybe party a little afterwards. Can't we just, be present in the present? I'm fielding interviews and sorting out my next steps. I don't want to make any permanent and financially significant decisions right this second."

"Yeah," I sigh. She's right. Fuck, I hate when I'm not. "You're right."

She grins. "I know."

Holding up my sake, I tap it against hers. "I can't wait to watch you walk across that stage," I tell her truthfully. "You're the first person in my life to graduate from a university. I'm proud of you, Stellina."

Her beautiful eyes meet mine. Glimmer. "And I'm proud of you. Proud of you for doing the work with therapy, for reaching out to Dex, for being here for me. And congrats on finishing your album."

I snort. She smiles that perfect fucking smile.

We eat dinner and go home.

We climb into bed, and I undress her slowly. Spend time memorizing the curves of her body. Palm her hips and thighs, squeeze her waist, kiss that delectable mouth. I savor every part of her I can, but I'm careful not to work us up too much. We still haven't gotten the green light on sex and while it's hard as hell to hold back, I keep telling myself that delayed satisfaction is a million times more fulfilling than instant gratification.

Besides, being forced to pull back has given me new insight on how special kissing can be. I'm so fucking present in the goddamn moment with her, I never want it to end.

After she falls asleep, I stare at the ceiling and panic rushes through me.

That's what I'm scared of. Not being in this moment. Losing her. Not having this, everything we've worked for, fought for, fucking bled for.

I can't lose my Stellina and the thought...it cripples me.

I work a swallow and turn on my side. I gather her in my arms and hug her to my chest. Her hair tickles my chin. She murmurs something nonsensical in her sleep.

I don't want to let her go. I don't want to not be with her. I can't lose her again because it would be like losing myself.

How many times have I gambled our future? How many times did I risk it all?

I don't want to do that again. But this time, she can't give me the reassurances. She won't put my mind at ease.

So it spins and swirls all night long.

Desperate thoughts. Needy emotions. Greedy want.

I sleep like shit, and the anxiety that builds in my body follows me throughout the following day, and the one after that. It clings to me like the fucking shadow I'm desperate to shake.

FOURTEEN
ALLEGRA

DEREK GRINS when I exit my bedroom, my graduation gown folded over my arm, my cap clenched in my hand. I smile and do a little curtsey, my white dress fluttering around my knees.

"You look beautiful, Stellina."

"Thank you!" I breathe in deeply. I feel beautiful today. Successful and accomplished and proud. "I can't believe today is graduation."

"I can," my brother replies, stepping out of his bedroom. He walks over and envelops me in a hug. "You've worked hard for this."

"Thanks, Levi." I rest my head on his shoulder as he tucks me under his arm. "I'm glad you're here."

"Me too, A." Levi glances at Derek. "You know my sister was valedictorian of her high school class?"

Surprise washes over Derek's face. "I didn't know that."

I flick my wrist dismissively. "It's not that big of a deal."

"Are you kidding?" Levi laughs. "It was a huge deal." He hugs me closer. "Mom and even Dad bragged about it for weeks."

At the mention of our parents, my smile slips and Levi's laughter cuts off. A heaviness descends on our shoulders, and it saddens me that we both bear the burden of our parents' rejection. Levi kisses my temple. "Mom would make a big deal out of today, too."

I dip my head in quiet acceptance. If she wasn't married to Dad, I think Mom would be proud of me too. Too bad she's not here to witness it.

"What time do you need to be at the stadium?" Derek asks, changing the subject. He absently spins his key ring on his finger.

I give Levi one last squeeze before slipping from his hold. "Not for a few more hours, but I'm going over to the girls' house. They're hosting a pre-grad soiree. A bunch of friends and mimosas and muffins. Nothing crazy."

"That's right," Derek says, as if remembering the plans I informed him of last week.

I grin. "See you at the stadium? Graduation is at 1 p.m.," I remind them.

Levi nods. "We'll be there."

"You need a ride?" Derek asks.

"No, thanks. I got one." I check my phone to see if he's here yet.

Derek's eyebrows furrow. "Who?"

I sigh. "Ethan."

"What the fu—"

"He's my friend, Derek. He's a really good friend," I cut him off.

Derek sighs. Levi chuckles.

My brother moves to the kitchen and pours himself a cup of coffee. Posting up against the kitchen island, he crosses one ankle over the other and watches as the tension between Derek and me mounts.

"I could take you," Derek asserts his point.

"I know. And I appreciate that. But this is my graduation," I remind him. "I want to be with my friends. We've been through a lot together. And I told you these plans last week."

"You didn't say Ethan was picking you up," he argues.

I shake my head, my frustration ticking up. Why is he making a big deal out of this? Why is he trying to make decisions about my friends and who I ride to a party with on my graduation day? "Originally, Nova's boyfriend—"

"The football player," Levi points out helpfully.

"West," I use his name, "was going to scoop me up on his way to Nova's. But his senior breakfast thing is running late so Ethan offered. It's not a big deal."

Derek's jaw clenches, a muscle pulsing in his neck, at my words. "Why make him come out this way?" Derek jangles his keys. "I'm right here and free to give you a ride."

Levi coughs to disguise his laughter.

I sigh, not nearly as amused as my brother. "Derek, don't you trust me?"

"Uh-oh," Levi murmurs.

"Mate, don't you have something to do?" Derek whirls on Levi.

"Nope." Levi shakes his head. He gestures toward us with his coffee mug. "Carry on."

Derek swears and grips the back of his neck. "Of course, I trust you, Stellina."

"Good. I trust you too." I pick up my purse and settle the strap on my shoulder.

"I just don't get why that guy has to give you a ride when I'm right here, wanting to drive you," Derek continues.

"Because that guy is my friend. And it's my graduation

day and I want to spend time with my friends without my boyfriend trying to control everything and make decisions for me," I snap back.

"Damn," Levi murmurs.

Derek's expression is stricken. An apology wells in my throat but I swallow it back down. As much as I love being with Derek, as much as I appreciate him coming back and caring for me, as happy as I am that we're together, sometimes, I need space. He barreled into town like a tornado, sweeping me up in his orbit the way he always does. And I love it. I love him.

But sometimes... "You've gotta let me breathe, Derek," I explain, drawing a boundary in the space between us. "I'm not going to crack," I say, wanting to put his mind at ease.

Yes, I needed him when I learned about the ectopic pregnancy. Of course, I've leaned on him. But his moving into my apartment, chauffeuring me home from the NGO each night, trying to buy us a home, and wanting to know all my thoughts for the future, has been a lot in a short amount of time.

Today, it's my graduation and I want to celebrate with my friends and have some fun like a normal college girl.

Anger twists Derek's mouth but his eyes look lost. Uncertain. He sighs again. "Okay."

I cross the room to give him a hug. "I love you. I'm happy you're here and coming to my graduation today."

He hugs me back and kisses my cheek. "I just worry, Allegra."

"I know. But I can make my own decisions and choices. If I need help, I'll ask."

Levi lopes out of the room. When his bedroom door closes, Derek wraps me in his arms and holds me close. He breathes me in for a few seconds and I melt against his frame.

"Happy graduation day," he says after a beat.

I smile against his neck, press a kiss there, and pull back. "See you at the stadium?"

He nods. "I'll be cheering louder than the other fuckers."

I laugh. My phone beeps, letting me know that Ethan is out front. I wave to Derek. "See you soon!"

Then, I bound down the steps and slip into the back seat of Ethan's waiting ride. Two other friends are in the car and we all exchange squeals of excitement as Ethan pulls away from the curb. He meets my gaze in the rearview mirror and winks.

"It's graduation day!" I yell out the wide-open window as the wind blows in.

My friends cheer as Ethan honks his horn in a staccato of celebratory beeps.

Right now, I don't know what the future holds, but I'm filled with hope. Possibility glimmers on the horizon and I want to reach for it with both hands.

I pull in a deep inhale and hold it in my lungs. The sunshine warms my skin and I smile.

Peace, contentment, and *knowing*—the good version—wraps around me.

"WE DID IT!" Nova fists pumps.

"Can you believe it?" Ivy asks, wide-eyed.

"Nope." Mckenna shakes her head. "I feel nauseous."

"Told you to take a shot," Nova points out. "Tequila settles nerves."

Mckenna gives her a look. Nova shrugs.

I sigh and glance out at the packed stadium. "Can you believe it? Four years of classes and homework, of highs and lows—"

"Of fucking Tinder," Nova comments.

"And softball." Ivy smiles softly.

"Internships," Mckenna points out.

"Friendship," I redirect the conversation.

The girls smile.

I laugh. "All of it, culminating in this moment."

Ivy exhales. "We did it."

I wrap my arms around Nova and Mckenna. Ivy does the same on the other side and the four of us form a huddle.

"Thanks for being my friends," Mckenna says, showing her sentimentality.

"Aw, Kenny. You're gonna make me cry," Ivy whispers.

"Don't!" Nova hisses. "Your makeup will run and I don't have time to fix it."

"Thanks for being my family," I tack on.

A tear slips down Ivy's cheek.

"Fuck," Nova swears.

We all laugh.

On stage, the ceremony commences.

"You ready?" Mckenna murmurs.

I bump my hip against hers. "Let's do it."

We give one last squeeze before lining up and walking into our graduation.

"CONGRATULATIONS!" Levi exclaims, clapping wildly when I meet him and our friends outside the crowded stadium.

Mav throws his arms around me. I hug him back.

"You did it," he whisper-hisses.

"Congrats, A." Jameson gives me a fist bump.

My brother kisses my cheek. "Do you feel smarter?"

"I've always been smarter than you," I remind him.

He chuckles. "And now you've got a fancy degree to back that up."

I swat at him, and his laughter grows.

"You're now the smartypants of the group," Mav tells me. He ruffles my hair and grins at me, his dimple popping. "Proud of you, A."

"Thanks for being here, Maverick." I give him a squeeze.

He scoffs. "Like I'd miss it. My name's not—"

"Too soon," Levi interjects.

Jameson snorts.

"Where's Derek?" I ask.

The group doesn't say anything and then, Mav grins.

"He's right there." Levi points.

I squint to see my guy walking toward me, a giant bouquet of wildflowers in hand.

"He had to bribe security to allow him to bring in the flowers," Jameson explains. "Apparently, all gifts are to be kept in cars for *after* the ceremony."

"Bribe security," Mav snorts. Lowering his voice, he murmurs, "They made him sign a piece of merch."

I giggle. My gaze turns back to Derek who is several strides away. A sexy smirk, brimming with pride, breaks out on his face.

I let out an exhale. Then, I rush him.

He moves the flowers to the side, so I don't crush them as I launch myself at him. Derek catches me with one hand, holding my body against his as my legs wrap around his waist.

He turns his head to kiss my lips. "Proud of you, Stellina," he whispers.

"You're here," I reply.

"Wouldn't miss this for the fucking world." His eyes are serious. He places me gently on my feet and presses the bouquet into my hands. "And I wouldn't *not* bring you flowers either. I want another date," he jokes.

I beam, cradling the bouquet in my arms.

"He just wanted to show the rest of us up," Levi calls out.

"Yeah," Derek agrees. "Where are your flowers?"

Mav flips him the bird.

Derek pretends to catch it and slip it into his pocket, like a kiss.

I laugh.

Derek's expression softens as he tugs on a strand of my hair. "I'm sorry. About earlier. I want you to enjoy being with your friends, Allegra. I just, hell," he sighs, "I worry."

I wrap my arm around his waist and lean into him. "I know. But today's a good day."

"Today's a great day," Derek agrees, holding me against his chest.

Dex steps beside him. "Want to keep the good times rolling?"

"You're here!" I gush, hugging him.

"Of course, I'm here. Wanted to see you get that diploma. Lord knows you earned it," Dex says, hugging me back.

"Thanks, Dex," I murmur.

He grins. "Anytime, A. Come on," Dex addresses the group, clapping his hands together. "Lunch and drinks at

Beirut." He winks at me. "Congratulations, Allegra. I always knew you'd turn it around."

I blush and dip my head. "Thanks to you."

Derek watches the exchange between us curiously.

"Nah." Dex waves a hand. "Because of you. Come on now. My treat."

The group turns toward the parking lot. Derek grips my hand.

I glance at him. "Yes," I answer his silent question. "This time, I'll ride with you."

Levi, Mav, and Jameson snicker as Derek flips them off.

I slide into the passenger seat of Derek's car and pull out my phone.

Me: Celebration at Beirut. Come!

Nova: Gah! After lunch? My dad is insisting on a French restaurant. Like he doesn't live in Paris...

Kenny: My parents are being weird.

Ivy: Weirder than usual?

Kenny: (eye roll emoji) As soon as I can get away, I'll be there!

Ivy: My cousins surprised me!

Me: Bring them!!

Ivy: Ha! If I can get a group consensus, we'll pass by.

Me: Nova?

Nova: Of course, I'm coming. My brothers are here too so after lunch with Dad, we'll roll through.

Me: Yay! We did it!

Ivy: Hell yeah, we did!

Nova: (four celebration emojis)

Kenny: (three heart emojis)

I grin and toss my phone into the cup holder. I'm excited to celebrate today with my found family, right here in LA.

FIFTEEN
DEREK

"WHAT DO YOU THINK?" I ask Maverick.

He gazes up at the beautiful, contemporary-styled home. It boasts an expansive lawn, a three-car garage, and a swimming pool with a swim-up bar, in the back.

His pale eyebrows draw together, and he chews the corner of his mouth.

"Shit," I mutter. "You don't like it."

"The place is beautiful." He surprises me.

"Right?" I chuckle, relieved Mav agrees.

"Could be in *Architectural Digest*."

"I know." I nod. "And it's not too much. It's not too flashy."

"Depends on who you ask..."

I look at him. He stares at me, as if waiting for some elusive puzzle piece to click into place.

Frustration coils in my gut. I've spent hours poring over home listings and have already had three conversations with my realtor Deb. "What? What's wrong with it?"

"Reign, nothing is wrong with the place. It's a gorgeous home," he repeats.

"Then, what's the issue?"

"The issue is...why are you house hunting for a home *for* Allegra, *without* Allegra?"

"I want to surprise her," I say defensively.

"I thought she was happy with the way things are?"

"She is. But at some point..." I trail off. I don't know how to explain to Maverick that I'm worried she's slipping away. That without a plan, without a future commitment, I'm...scared.

"The grand fucking gesture," Mav mumbles.

"What?" I look at him.

"It's about one hundred steps up from bowling," he carries on.

"So, she'll like it?"

Now, Mav sighs. "I don't think you should buy a place without talking to her. See what she wants, what style she likes, what neighborhood she sees herself in. Besides, where does she want to live? Or work?"

"You sound like Dex."

"Well, he sounds a lot more reasonable than you."

"Mav, if we're going to stay in LA, we need a place to live."

"You both have places to live," he points out, narrowing his eyes at me.

I heave out a sigh and look away. "I want to know that we're in this together."

"In what?" Mav's tone is quieter than it was a moment ago. "A relationship?"

"Just...life," I say. "I know Allegra is happy with how things are but for me, it's all unsettled. I don't know where we're going to live or where she's going to work. What we're going to do. What comes next, Mav?" I turn to ask my friend.

Maverick's face shudders, a shadow passing through his irises. "You enjoy the moment for the moment, Derek. You embrace what is and adapt to whatever comes next. You and Allegra, together."

I nod once, a curt movement. The same worry and anxiety that's followed me the past few weeks swells up my throat, coats the roof of my mouth, until I feel nauseous.

"Buying this massive house in this gated community, tucked away from her world, isn't going to change the way she feels about the future," he says quietly.

"I'm not trying to..." I trail off.

"Make decisions for her? Control the situation before she can?" he asks softly.

"Isolate her," I finish my sentence. But Mav's words reverberate in my mind, and I shake my head, hearing the point he's making. Understanding Dex's warning. "Fuck."

Mav tosses an arm around my shoulders. "It's a sick property. You've got good taste."

"What if she takes a job someplace else?"

"Then, you move."

"What if she doesn't want to take the next step with me? She says she does but...what's holding her back?" I confess my deepest worry about Allegra's and my relationship.

"You should talk to her," he calmly replies.

"And say what? I need to know what's next for you, so I know what's next for us? I don't like you working downtown near that park? I hate when I don't know where you are or who you're with?" I spit out, admitting the thoughts that fester in my mind. Dangerous, unpredictable, destructive thoughts.

Mav sucks his teeth. "Wouldn't lead with any of that."

I sigh.

Mav squeezes my shoulder. "Just sit down and talk to her, Derek. Calmy. Rationally. Like an adult."

"Fuck off."

He laughs. I glower.

"You need to be honest with her. Tell her how you're feeling. She'll hear you out. But..."

"But what?"

"But you've been hot and cold with her from the beginning, Reign. I know you don't want to hear it, but the truth is, there are two of you in this relationship and it can't always be on your terms. Let Allegra take the lead this time. Give her a chance to figure out what she wants. She's waited more than a minute for you to sort your shit out," he says gently. "This time, you can wait for her."

I sigh heavily. Mav shrugs.

Fuck. I hate when Maverick's right.

AS THE SUMMER stretches before us, I try to settle into a routine with Allegra. I wake up next to her each morning, hang out with her and her girlfriends, and swing by the NGO to pick her up in the evenings.

I take her to her final checkup with Dr. Davis, continue to look at properties for sale in the LA area, and meet Dex for burgers. I kick it with Levi, exchange emails with Sarah, songwrite with Mav, and take Johan up on his fucking offer to play golf.

The days bleed into each other. The nights are filled with wine and laughter. Allegra looks happier. The Clovers are in a good place, gearing up for our first live show since the tour. Things are falling into place and life is good.

A week after Allegra's graduation, Levi and Mav decide

to meet some friends to play poker. I beg off, preferring to wait for Allegra to finish her work at the NGO so we can eat dinner together.

I pick her up and we enjoy a delicious Italian meal with a generous glass of Cabernet Sauvignon. When we return to Allegra's, the condo is blissfully empty.

My girl gives me a salacious grin and a thrill runs up my spine. "Levi's out for the night," she murmurs, walking backwards toward her bedroom.

I smirk. "He'll be back. He's just playing poker."

Allegra cocks her head, studying me. "We've got time," she says huskily, raising her arms in the air.

My mouth grows dry at what she's offering. It's been so long. Over six weeks, while we've waited for her to be cleared by Dr. Davis. God, I've missed her. My eyes drink her in, lingering on her beautiful curves and dark eyes.

"Is it too soon?" I ask, even though my fingers are curled under the hem of her shirt and I'm peeling it up her sexy frame. I need this connection with her. This moment, this joining, to center me. I need her to remind me that we're going to be okay.

No matter what, it's me and her. Together.

I slow my movements, knowing I need to proceed cautiously. I need her words.

"Are you sure?" I whisper, dropping my mouth to her shoulder. I press a kiss there before sliding my lips up the column of her neck. My mouth lingers over the shell of her ear as I wait for her response.

She shivers, goosebumps breaking out over her skin. I move my hand over them, erasing them with the heat of my palm. "I'm sure."

"Fuck, Stellina," I moan, my hands sliding down her back to cup her denim-clad ass.

She tugs my shirt up and I lose it quickly. As my hands find her hips, she tilts her pelvis forward to brush against me. I nearly see stars. It's been so long and I've missed her so goddamn much. Her mouth finds mine as I hold her flush against me.

Our kiss is deep, filled with yearning and tenderness. Each brush of my lips over hers roots me to this moment and I never want to pull away. My fingers thread through her hair, holding her face, as I slant my mouth over hers. Our touches are intentional, memorizing, and languid.

She wraps her arms around my neck, leaning into my frame. The scent of her perfume, the feel of her hair against my skin, the little mewls that fall from her mouth, wash over me. Everything outside of Allegra falls away until she's all I can see, all I need. My palms track down her back, wanting to touch every inch of her. Slowly, I redirect us to her bedroom, never breaking our connection.

The door closes behind us and I sigh, pulling back only to drink her in. I remove her bra, sliding my palm down the valley in between her breasts. Her nipples pebble, desperate for my touch, for my mouth. I drop to my knees as I draw her closer, pulling one pert breast into my mouth and flicking my tongue over her sensitive bud.

"Ohh," she breathes, her hand catching the back of my head and holding me there.

Fuck, she's sweet.

As I give her other breast the same treatment, I pop the button on her jeans and drag down the zipper. Slowly, I roll her jeans over her hips, helping her step out of them when they pool around her ankles. Gripping the back of her thigh, I look up. Goddamn, she's sexy. Hooded eyes, swollen lips, and flushed cheeks, my girl nearly undoes me.

My love for her swells like a balloon, filling the dark,

empty spaces inside me. She makes me whole. My fingers tremble as I stroke the skin on the back of her leg.

She's standing before me, wearing only a tiny scrap of black lace, and — "You are everything, Allegra. Fucking perfection."

Her eyes hold mine and a shiver ripples over her body at my words, at the desire dripping from them.

Her hands dust over the ink that swirls up my arms before her fingers tighten on my shoulders. I drag my nose along her lower abdomen and playfully nip at her belly button.

She shudders again and I grin. I pull her thong to the side as my fingers dip inside.

My eyes hold hers as I swipe two fingers through her folds, already slick with want, with need, with anticipation. "Fuck, beauty," I groan, feeling her want coat my fingertips.

"I missed you," she admits.

"Jesus, love," I groan. "You have no fucking clue."

She tugs at me, urging me to stand. I kiss her hip before I force myself to my feet. Swinging Allegra into my arms, I carry her to bed, lay her out, and continue to explore her sexy body —a body that was fucking made for me—by kissing every inch of her skin with a tenderness that brings tears to her eyes.

"Don't cry, Stellina." I brush away a tear. Cupping her cheek, I angle her face so I can better read her eyes. "What's wrong, baby?"

"Nothing," she whispers. "I just, I need you, Derek."

I capture her mouth again and give her some of my neediness in return. "Always need you, beauty. Need this connection with you." My fingers caress her, my eyes drinking in each of her expressions.

I lose my pants and boxers before settling over her.

Then, I drag the head of my cock through her slick wetness, loving how she shudders and gasps. I rock into her so damn slowly, I'm scared I'm not going to last.

My beauty lifts her hips, meeting me as we come together. When I bottom out, we both sigh.

"I love you, Allegra," I tell her as I continue to rock against her. Pull out gently, slide back in. Set a pace that is more rhythm, music and fucking poetry, wrapping around us like the song I wrote for her.

I make love to my Stellina. I shield her body with mine and bring her to a peak that shimmers in its intensity, that envelops in its depth. My embrace cocoons both of us from the outside world. Our kisses are healing, our touches make us whole. Join us as one.

Forgiveness. Acceptance. Trust.

Once upon a time, we made a baby and didn't know it.

Tonight, we come together in a love so powerful, it renders me speechless. And I'm conscious of every second of it. I memorize it, breathe it in, lose myself in it.

Under my watchful gaze, Allegra comes apart like a shooting star.

I revel in it. Revel in her.

For the first time in weeks, I feel centered. Certain.

"Stellina," I howl, falling apart on top of her. My seed fills her empty womb and I know that one day, we'll make another baby. Our love will grow a whole family.

But it's too soon. Too much.

And yet, not nearly enough.

Allegra wraps her legs and arms around me, and I hold her against my chest.

"I love you, Derek," she pants in my ear.

I grip her hair and pull back to stare into her eyes. "You're my forever, Allegra."

Then, I kiss her hard and keep her close. When we drift off to sleep, I exhale into her hair and relax. My anxiety abates, my fear settles, and I trust in my connection with Allegra.

I decide to live in the moment, to take things as they come, to enjoy what is.

SIXTEEN

ALLEGRA

"READY TO PARTY!" Nova announces, raising a bottle of champagne in the air. She's wearing a short miniskirt and she shakes her ass like she's already had a few drinks.

Ivy rolls her eyes as Kenny pushes Nova into my apartment.

"Where's Levi?" Ivy asks.

"And Derek?" Nova tacks on, winking at me.

I laugh. "They're already at the venue. They got there early to set up and warm up. It's a small, local place. Not their usual scene but I think they're all feeling nostalgic."

"Are they happy they wrapped the new album?" Ivy asks. "Now, they can enjoy summer."

The girls enter my condo and drop their bags, some bottles of alcohol and mixers, and a few bags of chips on the kitchen table. It's a proper, newly-graduated-from-college girls' pregame, and seeing them fills me with another layer of excitement for tonight.

"Yes! I don't think they expected it to happen so quickly. Watching them record..." I pause, remembering the afternoons sitting outside the booth and staring at them, mesmerized. "It was wild. They were so in sync."

"They've been together a long time," Kenny points out.

"Yeah. I think sometimes they miss those early days though," I comment, thinking about Derek's desire to now buy a home. It's as if he's searching for something meaningful. A commitment to tie him down the way the Clovers once tied him to Boston.

But now, the guys could live anywhere in the world and meet up to record or go on tour. The need to be roommates, to constantly talk about music, to always be in the studio, isn't there. That sense of urgency has disappeared and with it, an entire outlook they prescribed to for years.

Ivy pops a bottle of bubbly and pours it into the champagne flutes Kenny passes to her.

"What's going on?" Nova lifts an eyebrow in my direction.

I sigh and plop down on a kitchen chair. "I want to go out tonight and have fun. Just, be in the moment, enjoy the night, be us."

"Okay," Nova agrees, always ready to party.

"But?" Kenny presses, taking the seat across from mine.

"Derek's been off lately," I lament.

"Off how?" Kenny asks.

"He wants to buy a house," I say, thinking about the conversations we've had the past few weeks. "It's like he wants our entire future hammered out so we can start making real decisions."

"A house!" Ivy exclaims.

"With like a lawn and a pool?" Nova digs for clarification.

I shrug. "He wants us to move in together and be...for real."

"You don't call this for real?" Ivy points around the open concept of Levi's condo. "You guys are living together in your bedroom after you lost a baby."

Kenny winces.

"I know," I admit slowly. I take a sip of champagne. "But buying a house is a big commitment."

"So is having a baby," Ivy murmurs.

"That wasn't a planned decision," I remind her.

"True," Nova agrees. "It happened and you were flying by the seat of your pants."

"Exactly! I feel like I've been on a roller coaster for the past year. Emotionally, mentally, even physically, I've been all over the place. Boston, LA. University, no university, enrolled part time again. With Derek, not talking to Derek, in love with Derek and planning a future. No baby, baby, loss of baby," I rattle off. "It's been...fuck, you guys, it's been a lot."

Nova drains half her flute in solidarity.

"It's been too much," Kenny agrees.

"What do you want, A?" Ivy asks thoughtfully. "Do you want to be with Derek?"

"Yes," I answer instantly.

"Do you want to stay in LA?" Nova poses.

"Yes. If I get a great job, doing something that matters to me, then yes," I reply.

"So...?" Ivy trails off.

I sigh. "I like how things are between Derek and me right now. We're...dating. Figuring things out. Not rushing them. I want to make sure we're making the decisions we're making for the right reasons and not because we're rushing into them or thinking we have to make them. You know?"

"You need more time," Mckenna deduces.

I nod. "I need more time."

"So, tell him that," Ivy says logically.

"I have. A few times. It's just…I feel like he needs more of a commitment from me," I voice.

Nova laughs. "Imagine that?" Her tone is sarcastic.

I grin.

"Guys suck," Ivy announces.

"Especially that Maverick." Mckenna shivers.

Nova rolls her eyes.

"I think you should just be honest with Derek," Ivy says. "Tell him what you need. I know he fucked up big time but the guy I've seen the past few weeks is all about supporting you and loving on you. Let him be that guy for a bit. You don't need to take on his needs in this moment. You're a great girlfriend, A. And he's trying his best." She shrugs. "Right now, that has to be enough."

"Yeah." Nova nods enthusiastically. "That's enough until you say it isn't."

"Until you decide you want more," Mckenna chimes in.

I grin at my girls. Standing from my chair, I wrap them in a hug. A big, messy group embrace. "Thanks. I don't know what I'd do without you girls."

"Me neither," Nova agrees.

We all laugh.

I sit back down. "I've got a few interviews lined up this week. If one of them works out…"

"You'll have more clarification," Ivy finishes my sentence.

"Exactly," I say.

"I can't believe you guys are going to hang out all summer without me," Mckenna whines.

Ivy shrugs. "Don't leave for Boston yet. Stick around longer."

Kenny sighs, worrying her bottom lip between her teeth. "Maybe I could stay until August..."

I wrap my arm around her shoulder. "Do it! You're going to do great in law school. Stick around and enjoy summer with us."

"I'll see," she murmurs.

"What do you have going on?" I ask Ivy.

"I'm hanging this summer," Ivy announces. "Then, I'll start working for my dad's company until I figure out exactly what I'm doing with my life."

"You'll figure it out," Mckenna says encouragingly.

I nod. "And you?" I glance at Nova.

She grins and bites her bottom lip. Always so coy. "I'm here for the summer. Then, I'm going to see my dad in Paris for two weeks. And then...I'm going to see what happens with West."

I gasp.

"Nova scored herself a football player!" Ivy cheers.

Nova's cheeks bloom with pink and I laugh. I've never seen Nova smitten before.

"It's serious," Ivy tells me.

Nova smiles. "We'll see what happens."

"I'm happy for you," I say.

She lifts her glass. "I'm happy for all of us. Now, let's party! And have some damn fun."

"Amen," Ivy seconds it.

Mckenna grins. "I'll stay until August."

We all squeal with excitement and lift our glasses, saying cheers to the evening.

To our futures.

THE VENUE IS small and packed with fans. Smoke gives the space a hazy, almost ethereal vibe. While most of the fans are corralled into the space in front of the stage, the girls and I are escorted to a table on a raised platform.

Bottle service awaits and one of the security guys lingers close by, keeping an eye on us.

"That was all Derek," Ivy murmurs.

"Or Mav," Nova points out.

Mckenna rolls her eyes and I grin. I have no idea why my unflappable friend is so salty toward Maverick Tate, but he's gotten under her skin.

We sit down and fix fresh drinks. The crowd grows rowdier, with cheers and applause ringing out.

I look up just as the Clovers take the stage.

Derek stares right at me. He kisses two of his fingers before pointing them in my direction.

"Aw," Nova gushes.

Women in the crowd let out a collective sigh, their eyes swinging toward me.

I blush and blow my guy a kiss.

Levi mutters something on stage and Maverick smacks him upside the back of his head.

"Good evening, LA!" Jameson bellows into the microphone.

The crowd goes wild.

Derek grins. "It's so damn good to be here."

"We missed you!" Mav tacks on.

"Thanks for coming out tonight," Levi says.

"We love you, Levi!" a fan hollers.

"We're proud of you!" another yells.

My brother dips his head, embarrassed. My chest squeezes for him. He's come a long way and it's wonderful to watch him step on a stage, sober, and connect with his fans in a meaningful way. In a way he'll recall tomorrow.

"I'm grateful to be here," Levi's voice echoes through the venue. "We don't do many shows like this anymore but this, tonight, with all of you, it feels right. Thanks for sticking by me."

"And thanks for showing up tonight," Mav adds, grinning until his dimple pops.

I swear a few women swoon.

"Have my babies, Maverick!" a woman in the front row yells.

Mckenna scoffs, her body growing rigid beside me.

"You ready for a show?" Derek redirects the conversation.

The crowd screams, their arms in the air, their bodies already dancing.

"Let's do it!" Jameson concludes.

The Clovers begin their first set and my friends and I watch, enraptured. Well, I am. I can't tear my eyes away from my rockstar. The one who has been my undoing from the first time he kissed me.

Tonight, he sings with so much soul, goosebumps dot my skin. I feel the gravel of his voice in the pit of my stomach, in the ache between my legs, in the pebbling of my nipples. I feel his words in the cavity of my chest, in the empty spaces he's been filling up, in the recesses of my mind.

None of these women hold a candle to a little star like you.

Sweet dreams, Stellina.

I love you, Allegra.

Emotion sweeps through me as I watch Derek perform. The music pours from him effortlessly, a gift he generously shares with everyone present. The band concludes their first set but before they take a break, my guy points at me.

"I got a special song for a special woman here tonight," he announces. "You guys have never heard it. No one, save for the band and her, have. So, you're fucking welcome."

More cheers. More clapping. More hollering about naughty, sexy things.

Derek grins. I laugh.

"Allegra Rousell, I fucking adore you," Derek says into the microphone. His head is cocked in my direction, his eyes locked on mine.

"Fuck, that's hot," Nova says, fanning herself.

"Here, have some water," Kenny advises, passing her a bottle.

The guys begin to play their instruments as Derek's voice—deep, husky, and undeniably sexy—rings out.

I stand transfixed as he declares his love for me before hundreds of fans. Before my brother, his bandmates, and my best girlfriends.

Before the world.

When he gets to the last verse, the space is quiet. Silent. Holding their collective breaths and watching him, captivated. I can barely breathe as I fall into his whiskey eyes and swim straight to his soul.

I love you more than the stars,
In spite of the loss,
Beyond the destruction.
You glow; I sear,
Together, we're too bright
To smother.
So I'll suffocate on our hurt,
And wrap you in my love,
Because, Stellina, it's always been you.

. . .

DEREK FINISHES THE LAST NOTE, and a beat of silence pierces the venue before raucous cheers explode, bringing down the house.

"Holy shit!" Ivy exclaims, her eyes wide when they meet mine. "That was...he was..."

"He's gonna buy you a house, baby!" Nova screams, her arms in the air.

Even Mckenna is laughing, pulling me into a side hug.

My girls envelop me, and I exhale. All the loss, the grief, the sadness. All the hope, the wishing, the wanting.

It leaves my lungs in a giant whoosh and the support of my friends buoys me until I find my footing again.

Then, I laugh. Loudly and deeply. All-consuming laughter that transports me to the past, connects me to the present, and colors my future in sunshine.

SEVENTEEN
DEREK

"YOU WERE AMAZING!" Allegra throws her arms around me.

In one movement, I've got her in my arms, her legs around my waist, my hand on her ass. I kiss her hard. "You're fucking incredible."

She laughs.

"Nice show, Derek," Dex's voice sounds out.

My girl slides down my body and turns toward Dex.

"Hey, Dex!" she exclaims, hugging him.

"Hey, A." Dex grins. "Thanks for the invite." His eyes hold mine and I duck my head in a nod.

It was cool to have him in the audience tonight.

"I hope you enjoyed the show," I mutter.

"Very much," he replies.

Nova watches our exchange with interest. "You are totally father and son. Men of few words, emotionally guarded."

Allegra blushes but Dex barks out a laugh at her assessment.

"You're right," he agrees.

I watch as Dex draws Allegra's friends into conversation. He congratulates them on graduation before extending congrats to the Clovers on a successful show.

He's comfortable and at ease. He jokes around. He exudes a confidence that's quiet but recognizable. The guys respect him; I can tell by how comfortable they are around him.

Levi and Dex exchange a few thoughts on rehab. Dex doles out some advice without sounding preachy. Mav makes him laugh. Jameson passes him a Coke.

And I hang back. I take it all in.

And for the first time in my life, I get to experience what it means to be proud of your parent. To be grateful for their existence. To enjoy their presence in your life.

"I liked tonight," Allegra murmurs, slipping her arm around my waist.

I drape my arm over her shoulders. "Tonight was special."

She glances up at me. "Thanks for singing my song."

I dip my face to hers and kiss her in response. "Want to go home now?"

She shakes her head. "Not yet. Let's celebrate."

I grin. "Okay."

Mav rallies our crew, and we head to a club downtown. I don't know when Mav arranged it, but the private area is already rented out and prepared to host us. As we gather in the space, an eclectic mix of musicians, friends, family, and Allegra and her girls, I look around and take it all in.

It's been years since we made it big and yet, tonight feels like one of those early days. It's exciting and new again. It holds the possibility of the unknown. A flare filled with hope.

Allegra wraps her arms around my waist. "Dance with me?"

I fold my arms around her to hold her close. "Of course." I sway with her in my arms.

Around us, drinks are poured. Cheers are exclaimed. Conversations break out in pockets.

But none of it matters. None of it registers.

I'm here with Allegra and that's enough.

It's everything.

And I won't fucking lose it again.

I'M desperate for her by the time we make it to my condo. Tonight, we let Levi have the place to himself. Instead, we're in my space and we're alone.

"Want you," she murmurs as I pull her sexy tank over her head.

"You got me," I remind her, unzipping her miniskirt. It falls to the floor, and she steps out of it.

I swear, drinking in her perfection. She's wearing red lace and fuck if she's not the hottest woman I've ever seen.

"Your turn," she giggles.

I grip the material of my shirt at the base of my neck and tug it off in one pull, discarding it. Allegra's hands are on my pants, unbuttoning my jeans, pushing them past my thighs, and cupping me through my boxers. She presses down, dragging the heel of her hand against my erection and I jerk against her. "Jesus."

"You're already hard for me," she comments as I shake off my jeans.

I place my hand on top of hers and grind into her palm. "I'm always fucking hard for you."

She laughs.

But there's nothing funny about this moment.

I can't tear my eyes from her. My hands tingle with energy. Usually, it signals a need to create. To write music.

Tonight, it's a need to touch her. To feel and caress and hold. My fingers brush along the tops of her shoulders, moving her hair behind her back. Her silky tresses slide over the back of my hand. My brunette beauty.

"I like it like this." I tug on the ends.

She lifts her face to mine, her hands glide over my hips to grab my ass. She steps into me until my cock drags along her abdomen.

I lace my fingers through her hair, drop my mouth to hers, and kiss her. It's deep and sensual. Her breasts push into my chest as I slide my tongue inside her mouth. Our lips move over each other's like whispers. Sweet nothings and naughty confessions. Promises and desires.

Our kissing turns to nipping. Our caresses grow needier. I back my beauty up until we're pressed against a bookshelf in my living room. They're built-ins, filled with shit I've never read but it looks good. Smart.

"Turn around," I command.

She shivers but does as I say. My eyes automatically drop to her ass, two sweet globes partially concealed by lace I want to rip off with my teeth.

"Fuck, beauty." My hand traces the curve of one cheek. I grab a handful and squeeze as she pushes back against my touch.

Stepping into her, I press my chest into her back and slide my hand around to slip two fingers beneath the lace between her thighs.

My fingers find her arousal and I suck in an inhale as she lets out a moan.

"You're already soaked for me, baby," I murmur in her ear as my fingers draw soft circles over her clit.

"Always wet for you, Derek," she tosses my words back in my face.

I smile and press a kiss behind her ear.

"You want my cock?" I ask, playing with her pretty pussy. Light, slow touches that cause her to shudder and moan my name.

"So badly," she pants.

I drag my fingers through her folds and insert two inside her, curling my fingers.

She gasps and bucks, her ass connecting with my rock-hard cock. She grinds her sexy ass against me.

I pump my fingers in and out.

"I want all of you," I tell her.

"Me, me too," she manages.

"Mm..." I nuzzle my cheek into her neck. "Look at me, beauty."

She glances at me over her shoulder. Fucking bedroom eyes with a greedy glint.

I turn her back around, so she's facing me. Then, I reach behind her, push a whole fucking stack of books to the floor, and perch her on the edge of the built-in. I set her right there. It's a tight squeeze but we make it work.

Dropping to my knees, I spread her legs, my hands big on her inner thighs. I sit on my haunches and grin at her wickedly.

"Touch yourself, Stellina," I demand.

"What?" she gasps, her eyes finding mine.

I take one of her hands and place it over the scrap of lace. "Show me how you want me. Pretend it's me." My voice is barely audible. With my hand on hers, I guide her fingers over the seam of her panties.

She groans, her hips lifting slightly to feel more pressure.

I move her fingers over the little nub filled with sensations to make her see stars. We rub slowly, lightly at first. Then, she increases the pace, her chest rising more frequently.

I remove my hand and just watch her. Take in the pink in her cheeks. The lust in her eyes. The soft swells of her pretty tits.

"Fuck," I swear. Unable to wait any longer, I lunge for her.

I pull her toward me before laying her out on my fucking coffee table. In the middle of the goddamn living room. With books littering the floor.

I snap the lace at her hip. Her pussy is perfect. Pink and swollen and glistening with her arousal.

Dropping back between her thighs, I drag my tongue up her core.

"Derek," she cries out.

My hand plants on her thigh. Holding her in place, I lap at her like a fucking animal. Needy, desperate, nearly feral in my desire to have her. Taste her. Fucking devour her.

Our intimacy turns full-on sexy. Angsty. Debased.

My fingers pump into her, my tongue swirls and sucks at her clit, and she unravels on my coffee table.

"Derek!" she hollers again, hooking one leg over my shoulder and digging her heel into my back.

I don't stop. I'm relentless.

She shatters. A long, gasping, heaving orgasm that has her fist colliding with my shoulder.

"Fuck! Jesus!" she cries out.

I lap at her until her body stops quaking. Then, I lift my head and smile.

"You ready for me, beauty?"

She widens her legs, dropping her knees to the sides in response. "I'm always ready for you, you fucker."

I laugh. Grab her chin in between my fingers, and kiss her hard, letting her taste herself on my tongue.

Then, I enter her. In one sharp thrust, I fill my beauty to the fucking hilt.

I pull back and stare at her. "Christ, you drive me crazy. Do you have any idea how badly I want you? Want a fucking future with you. I want a life with you, Allegra. I want our baby. I want it fucking all."

Her eyes widen as she grasps my shoulders and stares at me.

I still inside of her. My chest heaves as I try to regulate my breathing. My hand curls around her side as I hold her in place.

"Tell me what you need," I demand.

"You. I need you. All of you. Like this," she says.

I swear, dropping forward to take her mouth again. We kiss, soft and slow and sweet.

Then, I fuck her. Hard and wild and savage.

I thrust into her deeply, feeling her sweet pussy clench me like a vise. Allegra cries out, arching up as her back comes off the table. I grip her hip and grind into her, my vision blurring as my body clenches.

"Gonna come, baby," I warn her.

"Me too!" She claws at my back.

"Get there, beauty. Fuck, love, get there."

"I'm coming!" she announces, her pussy tightening around my cock.

"Shit," I swear as I start to spill inside of her.

One more thrust and...

She drops and I collapse on top of her, the legs of the coffee table finally giving way.

"Ouch! Shit," Allegra swears as the wood buckles and we land in a heap on top of the table.

"Can't stop," I laugh, as I continue to come inside her delectable body.

She's laughing. Her arms wrap around me and gather me to her chest.

My hips tilt forward one more time, until I finally reach the end of my release.

Grabbing her, I hug her tight. Hold her close. The coffee table is flattened beneath us.

"You okay?" I ask, pulling back to make sure she's not injured.

She's laughing so fucking hard, little tears are streaming from the corners of her eyes. "Holy shit! We broke the table."

I slap one hand down next to her head and push myself up. Glancing at the wreckage around us, my body begins to shake with laughter. It bursts out of me loudly. Uninhibited.

"Only you can make me lose my fucking mind like that," I promise.

She beams. "Better than breaking the bed."

I snort.

And then, we crack up all over again.

Our bodies tremble as we howl. As our laughter subsides, I scoop up my Stellina and walk into the bathroom.

Flipping on the showerhead, I wait for the water to run hot before I step inside with her in my arms. I set her on her feet and our eyes catch. She smiles. I grin. And the moment between us stretches into an eternity.

Acceptance. Forgiveness. Love. Home.

I squirt body wash onto a loofah and drag it over Allegra's body. As I wash her, care for her, show her how much she means to me, I settle an internal debate.

I'm buying us a fucking home.

"YES, I'll be home in time for dinner," I promise Derek as I shuffle through a file on my desk.

"Let's do takeout. Chinese, Italian, or Greek?" he offers.

"Greek," I decide. "Can you get spanakopita?"

"Obviously."

I laugh before I sigh. The piles of folders on the desk are reaching new heights. Even though I've been spending as much time at the NGO as possible, my study sessions leading up to finals, coupled with graduation festivities, meant less hours. Subsequently, there is now more work. The new hire from New York has been delayed and in the interim, things are piling up. "I gotta go if I'm going to make it home in time. There's a mountain of folders I want to get through today."

"Okay," Derek says. "I can come pick you up in thirty?"

"Don't worry about it. I have my car today. Enjoy hanging at the studio," I reply, shaking my head at Derek's constant worrying.

"We may have a new single," he says proudly.

"Happy recording!"

"All right, beauty. See you later."

"Love you," I murmur, loving that I can say it whenever I want now. Without hesitation. Without second-guessing myself.

"I love you, Stellina," Derek replies.

In the background, I hear Maverick make a gushy *aw* sound followed by kissing noises. Derek swears at him.

I laugh. "'Bye."

"Later, love." Derek disconnects the call.

I toss the phone down on the desk and get to work. The office is unusually quiet today. Two of the staff are working a fundraising initiative downtown. I turn on a Spotify playlist and dig into the first folder. As I focus on the paperwork requiring my attention, I tune everything else out.

When I stand up to stretch and use the bathroom, I'm shocked that nearly three hours has passed. I glance at my phone and wince when I note the time. If I don't leave now, I'm going to blow Derek and dinner off.

I hurry to the bathroom, reapply my makeup, and fluff up my hair. Then, I snap the folder on my desk closed, organize my notes for tomorrow, and grab my purse.

I'm exiting the building, rooting around in my purse for my keys, when a man's voice calls out.

"Hey!"

I turn, my lips parting to ask him if I can help him.

Before I can get any words out, he's barreling into me. The stench of his breath, cigarettes and alcohol, washes over me seconds before the back of my head slams into the concrete and his heavy body lands on mine.

"Get off me!" I shriek, flailing beneath him.

His hair is long, swinging forward into his wild eyes. He cinches both my wrists easily and slams them over my head, shredding the skin on my knuckles. I buck up against him and he growls. Releasing one of my wrists, I move to slap him, but he beats me to it.

His hand cracks against the side of my face and I see stars. A whole night sky of tiny, twinkling lights.

"Get off!" I shout again. Panic blares in my mind as adrenaline spikes in my bloodstream. I fight him, desperate to be free of his hold.

He reaches for my purse, a few feet away on the ground. My keys and phone have spilled out. My day planner is open, a sticky note catching the wind and blowing away. Pens, lip gloss, hair clips. It's all in my peripheral vision as his weight pins me to the ground.

He scampers over to my possessions, his eyes scanning them greedily as I suck in an inhale. My heartbeat is erratic, and my limbs feel weak. Shaky.

I scurry to my feet and a wave of nausea slams into me. Dizzily, I reach out, my fingertips grazing the brick of the building.

The guy must sense my escape because he pivots on his foot. His expression is blank, his eyes simultaneously unhinged and empty. A shiver works over my skin as I hunch forward.

This time, I see his fist coming, but my response time is delayed. I'm too slow.

He catches me in the ribs, and I grunt, the air leaving my lungs in a whoosh. Panicking, I try to breathe in, but the oxygen won't come. My lungs drag in wisps of fear.

Is he going to knock me out? Hurt me? Or worse? A shiver rolls through my limbs.

My palm slips over the brick and I crumple, my knees hitting the pavement. His hand connects with my face again, this time splitting my lip. I fall forward and lie there.

I don't move, for fear of what that will mean. Instead, I

focus on breathing. I pull in a shallow breath, followed by a longer one. In my peripheral vision, I see him scoop up my keys and phone and wallet. Watch as he shoves them into my purse. Note that he doesn't bother glancing around to see if anyone saw him rob me.

It doesn't matter. He's past caring.

He doesn't look back to see if I'm moving. Or hurt. Or breathing.

Maybe he doesn't remember me at all.

I close my eyes as he runs across the street. I lie there, on the cracked asphalt, and block out the pain blooming in my cheek, pulsing in my head, throbbing along the side of my body.

Then, I drag myself to my hands and knees. Blood drips from my lip—or maybe my nose—onto the pavement. I watch it fall and seeing it, thick and crimson, gives me the surge of energy to get to my feet.

A group is huddled in the corner of the park, but they ignore me. Wary and on edge, I limp to the end of the road. I stumble on the corner. The headlights of the oncoming traffic are distorted, causing my head to spin.

"Hey! You all right?" a woman hollers.

I look up and squint. A woman comes into focus. She's driving a bus. She's leaning closer to the open double doors and staring at me wide-eyed.

"You need to go to the hospital," she commands.

I try to nod.

"Fuck, girl. He fucked your face." A man moves off the bus toward me and I flinch. "It's all right. I'm not gonna hurt you." He holds up both hands, palms open.

Another woman appears. Her expression is tight, her eyes sympathetic. "Come on, honey. Let's get you on the bus. We'll take you to the hospital."

I nearly sigh in relief at the sight of her. This woman, this stranger. But her eyes are kind. Her touch on my elbow is gentle. At her presence, my exhaustion surges and I nearly collapse.

The guy catches my weight. "Got you, girl." He hoists me up and directs me onto the bus.

It starts with a lurch. Stop and go. I don't know how long it takes to arrive at the hospital. I just know I vomit into a plastic bag twice on the way there. When we arrive, the kind woman and the strong man assist me to emergency. They point to the bus and explain the situation before leaving me in the capable hands of a nurse.

Understanding washes over her face when she takes in my injuries.

She whisks me into triage, skipping the ER waiting room entirely. I'm now one of the more pressing emergencies. Her hands are cool and clinical as they move along my face, the back of my skull, check my ribs. I wince but don't cry.

It's as if I'm watching her check me over. It's an out-of-body experience and even though I feel her touch, it doesn't register. Everything hurts and yet, I can't respond to the pain. Emptiness claws at my throat even though I desperately want to scream.

"Is there someone we can call for you?" Her voice is measured.

I force my eyes to hers. They're green. "You have pretty eyes."

She smiles lightly. "We can call anyone you'd like."

I sigh. Squint as if it will help me recall his number. For a moment, my home phone number, from my parents' house, floats through my mind.

If I called Mom, would she come? Would Dad let her?

"If you prefer to be alone, that's—"

"I know a number," I mumble. I ask her to look up the number to Hendrix's recording studio.

She looks at me like I'm not making sense but agrees to give the studio a call. When she leaves, a different nurse, followed by a doctor enter.

They ask about my injuries. They inquire if I need a rape kit. They're calm and direct. Well versed in the spiel they're laying out. I open my mouth and everything I remember pours out in a monotonous, robotic voice that doesn't sound like mine.

"It was a simple robbery," I say. "I work for a homeless-ness NGO downtown. Well, intern."

The doctor nods sympathetically while the nurse jots down notes.

"You can press charges," the doctor says.

"Against whom?" The man who attacked me was most likely on drugs. Or suffering from mental-health issues. He may not even remember coming at me. "I don't remember what he looks like."

The doctor frowns. "Are you sure?"

I recall his stringy brown hair and empty blue eyes. "I'm sure."

She sighs. "Okay. I'm going to stitch up your lip. Your face is swollen and will bruise on the right side, and you have a concussion. We're going to X-ray your ribs, but I'm certain there are fractures. Once we know the severity, we can talk about treatment. For now, I'd like you to sit up." She props more pillows behind my back. "And tell me if you have shortness of breath or any severe pain."

I exhale. Pain cuts through my side. "Okay," I agree.

She sits next to the bed and tilts my chin to get a better

look at my face. "The cut isn't horribly deep. I'm going to use stitches that will dissolve."

"Thank you," I murmur.

"You're handling the pain quite well."

"I mostly feel numb."

She frowns. "You sure this was a random attack? If it was someone you know or—"

"It wasn't," I cut her off. I'm not the victim of a domestic abuse situation. This was a wrong place, wrong time, scenario.

She doesn't reply but begins to stitch my lip.

I don't move. Or cry. Or even blink.

NINETEEN
DEREK

"I GOTTA GO!" I tell Mav, tilting my head toward the door. "I called in our order over thirty minutes ago."

"George's Greek isn't going to give it away," Mav argues, pulling up the clip he wants me to watch. He has an idea for the cover of our new single. "It's only two minutes long."

He thrusts his phone in my hands. I tap play and watch the video, feeling the edgy vibe of the beer commercial.

"It's a cool vibe," I agree.

"It's a sick vibe," he kicks it up a notch.

I laugh. "Bro, I'm cool with it. Share your ideas with Claire. Make a fucking mood board. Run with it."

Mav rears back, surprised. "Seriously?"

"Yeah." I clasp his shoulder. "I trust you, man. Do you." I shoulder my backpack. "Now, I really gotta—"

"Derek!" Henny rushes into the small kitchen attached to the studio.

I freeze at the thread of panic in his tone. Hendrix is laid-back. One of the calmest dudes I know. For him to be visibly worried has my nerves on high alert.

"What's wrong?" I ask, a sense of déjà vu, quickly followed by sheer terror, rushes through me.

Mav is still beside me, his gaze trained on Henny.

The temperature in the small space, usually stuffy, plummets.

"It's Allegra," Hendrix breathes out. "The hospital called and—"

"The hospital?" Mav asks.

"She was attacked," Hendrix supplies.

"Attacked?" The blood drains from my face. My hands curl into fists as I try to steady the tremble of my fingers. "What the fuck does that mean? How bad? Is she—" Anguish cuts my tone. "Is she hurt? Fuck, of course she's hurt. The hospital…" I trail off, trying to make sense of what Hendrix is telling me.

"Which hospital?" Mav asks.

"What's going on?" Levi barrels into the cramped space.

Mav cuts him a look. "It's A." His voice is quiet.

Fear floods Levi's expression. Jameson steps up behind him.

Hendrix swears. "She's at St. Clara's, downtown. The nurse said a bus dropped her off."

"A bus?" Levi asks, bewildered.

"Let's go," I command, rushing the door.

"I'll drive." Jameson is right behind me. He pulls my backpack from my shoulder and rifles inside for my keys. I let him because my head is too fucked up to drive. My mind is all over the damn place.

Someone hurt my girl.

Someone put his fucking hands on her.

The hospital.

Hurt. Alone. A goddamn bus.

I slide into the passenger seat of my Camry. Levi and

Mav pile into the back seat. Jameson pulls away from the curb. We sit in silence, without music, as the car speeds toward the hospital.

My heart thuds in my temples. My stomach is slick with worry. My throat choked with emotion. That anger I used to feel in an instant is dormant. Instead, it's snuffed out from straight-up panic for my Stellina. For her well-being. I need to see her, hold her, care for her.

I need her more than I need to seek revenge on the fucker who hurt her.

That will come afterwards. Right now... "Fuck," I swear out loud.

No one responds.

Jameson drops us at the front of emergency. "I'll park and meet you in there," he says.

Mav, Levi, and I rush from the car and into the hospital. We skid to a stop in front of reception.

I open my mouth to bark questions at the nurse, but Maverick steps in. Leaning closer, he lowers his voice and explains our situation.

Her gaze darts to me, then Levi, before settling on Maverick. Recognition flares in her eyes and my heart sinks. If she asks for a fucking autograph, I'll lose my goddamn mind.

"Right this way," she says instead, surprising me.

The nurse leads us to a secluded waiting room and I'm relieved to have a moment of privacy. A second to pull myself together before I barrel into Allegra's room.

The doctor appears a moment later. She sizes us up. "Which one of you is Derek?"

I step forward. "I am."

She nods. "I'm Dr. Reese. Allegra has been asking for you."

"I'm her boy—fiancé," I lie, in case there's some bullshit family rule.

The doctor doesn't reply but from her expression, I know she knows I'm lying. I mean, technically. But, one day, I will be Allegra's fiancé.

"I'm her brother." Levi steps up beside me.

"Her best friend." Mav raises his hand.

Dr. Reese nods again. Her eyes cut back to me. "She's asking for you."

I glance at Levi.

His expression is unreadable, but he shoves me forward. "Go." His eyes meet mine. In them, I read acceptance.

Without overthinking it, I reach out and pull him into a hug.

He smacks my back. "Go. She needs you."

"Thank you," I tell him, thanking him for so much more than this moment. Déjà vu rocks through me again, momentarily disorienting, and I shake my head to clear the dizziness. It feels like we've been here before. And chance dictates we shouldn't be back here again. Not this soon. Not like this.

I follow the doctor toward the double doors that lead to a hallway of patients' rooms.

"A nurse will be out in a moment to explain Allegra's care," the doctor says over her shoulder.

We enter the long hallway and she leads me to Allegra. "She's resting," she cautions. "She's okay. But she has a pretty severe concussion. Two of her ribs on the right side of her body are fractured. One is badly bruised. Her lip is stitched up and the side of her face is swollen."

I pull in a sharp inhale as she explains Allegra's injuries.

I don't know what I expected but hearing them laid out like a grocery list pulls me up short.

I glance at the doctor. "Who was he?"

She shakes her head. "I don't know."

I close my eyes for a moment. "Will she be okay?"

"Yes. She'll heal."

"I mean emotionally. Mentally."

Dr. Reese regards me with a look I can't decipher. "I hope so."

Fuck. "Me too."

"She's in here." The doctor touches the doorframe to room 204.

"Thank you, Doctor," I say.

She nods before continuing down the hallway.

I stand outside Allegra's room for a second. Draw in a deep breath. Blank my expression. Then, I knock lightly and push inside.

She turns and meets my eyes as I enter.

The emptiness in them plunges into my chest like a knife.

Her eyes widen.

My heart breaks. I stride to her side and drop to the floor. My knees hit the tile and the jarring sensation pulses up my body, slamming into my throat. I barely feel it. I carefully reach for her hand. "Stellina."

"Derek," she breathes out. She slides her hand out from underneath mine and I hate the red scrapes that mar her knuckles. She grasps the back of my head and pulls me closer, and I go willingly, laying my head on her chest as she cradles me.

I should be comforting her but right now, she's holding on to me for dear life, and I need it. I need her.

The urge to run, to take off and clear my mind, to track down the fucker and ruin his life, all take a back seat to her. To being with her, having eyes on her, caring for her.

Again, I don't want to run as much as I want to stay. Need to fucking stay.

"You're here," her voice cracks.

I look up. "Of course, I'm here."

A small smile tilts the corner of her mouth. "I was so scared."

"I'm so fucking sorry, beauty."

"But I did it. I got myself here."

"I know. You're brave, Allegra. So fucking strong."

A tear forms in the corner of her eye. "I might be broken."

"You're perfect," I refute her statement.

"I'm tired."

"Then sleep, my love."

She blinks slowly. "Will you stay?"

"I'm not going anywhere," I promise.

"Because I'm exhausted. And too scared to close my eyes." Her voice is a whisper, sleep already dragging her under.

I cup her uninjured cheek. "I'll watch over you. Sleep, beauty."

She closes her eyes. Her jaw relaxes. Her head turns, resting in my open palm.

I study her split lip. Her bruised cheek. Her scraped hands.

Fury rolls through my veins. Anger beads in my blood. Pure hate pulses in my temples. I want to destroy the man who did this to my Stellina.

Instead of reacting to the overwhelming emotions coursing through me, I take a deep breath. I shift to sit on the chair beside Allegra's bed.

I pull out my phone and text the guys to let them know that Allegra's sleeping. To inform them that I'm not leaving her fucking side. To tell them that she's in room 204 if they want to pop their heads in but not to disturb her.

They come by to check on her. Levi looks crushed. Mav appears sickened. Jameson is withdrawn.

We all share a heavy look. Anger and anguish.

"You can't all be in here," a nurse warns. "She needs her rest."

Levi cuts me a look. I arch an eyebrow.

He sighs. "Call me when she wakes up."

"Promise," I swear.

Mav and Jameson dip their heads. The three guys leave me with Stellina as I keep watch over her.

I listen to the evenness of her breathing. I watch the monitor that keeps track of her heartbeats. I study her beautiful face as she sleeps.

When she whimpers in her slumber, I place a hand on her chest. Immediately, she calms, quiets, and falls back into her dreams.

It soothes me just as much as her that I can provide her reassurance. That I can comfort her. That I am the man she needs in this moment. More than enough.

I don't know how many hours pass. The nurse comes in several times to check on Allegra. She administers pain meds through an IV. Takes her temperature and checks her vitals.

When I feel myself start to doze off, I stand, stretch my legs, and call Dex.

"Hey!" He picks up on the first ring.

"Dad." The word shoots out of my mouth without my thinking it. It feels natural. Normal. Surprise rocks through me.

He's quiet for a beat. "You okay, son?"

Fuck. My throat squeezes. Emotion rolls through me. I clear my throat. "Allegra's in the hospital."

"What happened? Is she okay?" Worry laces his tone.

I exhale. "She was attacked."

"What hospital? I'm on my way." In the background, I hear the jangle of his keys.

I rattle off the information. Twenty minutes later, my father walks into Allegra's hospital room with a tray of coffees and a bag of doughnuts. He places a chair beside mine and sits down quietly.

For several long moments, we stare at Allegra's sleeping form.

Then, Dex takes a swig of his coffee and glances at me. "Close your eyes for a few, Derek. I'll watch over her."

My eyes burn even as I try to protest his suggestion. "I—"

"I promise to wake you the second her eyelashes flutter," he swears.

I snort, but the drag of sleep pulls harder at his words. At his presence. "You won't leave?" I ask, staring at my Stellina.

"I'm not going anywhere," he promises.

"Okay," I agree. I scoot my chair closer to Allegra's bedside so I can hold her hand.

Then, I let my eyes drift shut. I let my father watch over us both.

And for the strangest fucking reason, I'm not as scared anymore.

TWENTY

ALLEGRA

"HOW DO YOU FEEL?" Dr. Reese asks the following morning.

"Like I was attacked," I admit. I try to sit up straighter and groan as my ribs protest in pain.

"How's your head?" she asks, feeling the back of my head for the bump that protrudes there.

"Throbbing."

"And your lip?"

"Sore."

She nods. "You've sustained some injuries, but given what occurred, you're lucky, Allegra."

Derek glowers. "Lucky? She could've been raped!"

Dr. Reese inhales sharply.

I reach for Derek's hand and squeeze. "It could have been much, much worse."

"Yes," Dr. Reese agrees softly. "Your concussion, and your ribs, will take time to heal. Be easy with yourself. I've spoken with Derek, as well as with your brother, and it seems like you'll be in capable hands at home."

Derek grunts. His expression is cool, his mouth pressed

in a thin line. Every time he meets my eyes, I read the fury, the agony, in his.

"I can't wait to sleep in my own bed," I agree.

"You'll have to remain sleeping upright for a few weeks," she cautions, pointing toward my ribs. "They'll take at least six weeks, if not longer, to heal."

"I miss my sheets," I tell her.

She chuckles. "I'll get your discharge papers ready to go. See if we can get you out of here in an hour or two." She glances at Derek. "In the meantime, Allegra has visitors."

"Okay," he says.

She lifts an eyebrow.

"I'm not going anywhere," he mouths off.

I expect Dr. Reese to push back but she chuckles. "Good for you." She turns to look at me. "If you get tired—"

"I'll kick them all out," Derek cuts her off.

"See that you do," Dr. Reese replies. "I'll pop back in before you leave." Placing a clipboard underneath her arm, she leaves my room in confident, measured strides.

I roll my head along the pillow and glance at Derek. "You can go get some rest," I say, noting the exhaustion that lines his face. "I'll be home soon."

"I'm right where I want to be," he replies, shifting closer to my bedside.

"Derek," I murmur, reaching for his hand.

He slips his fingers in between mine.

"You could shower. Change. Eat," I say.

He shakes his head. "None of that matters."

I snort. Wince. "I promise I'm fine if you—"

"I'm not," he interjects.

"What?"

"I'm not fine. Fuck, Stellina, my heart fucking skipped out of my body when Hendrix told me you were attacked."

His fingers clutch mine tighter. "I just, I need to be here with you. Keep my eyes on you. I'm still too...rattled."

"Okay," I say lightly. His words are a salve to old wounds, emotional ones, that he can't see. At the sincerity in his eyes and the angry twist of his lips, a strange sense of relief flows through me. I feel safer, stronger, knowing that he's here.

He dips forward and brushes a kiss over my forehead. He lingers for a moment, and I breathe him in. Tilt my face up to meet his lips.

He smiles but pulls back. "Your lip."

"It's fine," I breathe out.

Derek chuckles. "You just said it's sore. I don't want you to hurt, beauty. I can barely handle seeing you in pain right now."

I sigh, annoyed that he won't oblige me and kiss me senseless. Still, at the tightness in half of my face, I know he's right. Kissing will be painful right now.

"Want me to let your fan club back?" he asks. "Not all at once. But a few at a time?"

"Who's here?"

"Who isn't here is the question you should be asking." He smiles. "Ivy, Nova, Kenny. Levi, Mav, Jameson. Dex."

"Dex!"

"He sat with me last night," Derek says, surprising me.

My mouth drops opened. "He did? How was it?"

Derek drops his head sheepishly. "It was...nice. Normal."

I squeeze his hand. "Good. I'm happy for you, Derek."

"Yeah," he agrees before changing the subject back to our friends. "Hendrix, fucking Ethan—"

I laugh. He rolls his eyes.

"Ethan's been a good friend to me this year," I remind

him. While we don't hang out regularly, we still check in with each other from time to time.

"And a girl named Devy," Derek adds.

"We worked together at Beirut," I explain.

"Dex told me. You want to see them before Dr. Reese cuts you loose?"

"Yes," I say. Knowing my friends are in the waiting room gives me a rush of energy. I want to see them. I want to thank them and show them that I'm okay.

Before Derek can text anyone and tell them to come back, a knock sounds on the door.

Derek turns and I glance up as my mother peeks into the room. I inhale sharply.

Her eyes find mine. A cloudy blue filled with pain. Regret. Apology. And hope. Her shoulders roll forward, as if to ward off witnessing my injuries. She steps into the room and horror crosses her expression.

My mouth drops open. Surprise slams into me as I grip the handrail on the bed.

Levi enters the space behind her.

Mom's face crumples as she looks me over. "My God, Allegra." A tremor threads through her tone and her hand comes up to cover her mouth.

Derek stands, positioning himself at my side. He slides his hand over mine.

"Mommy," I breathe, my voice breaking.

Mom steps forward. Tears flood her eyes. Her hand shakes as she reaches for me.

I loosen my hold on the handrail and Derek slips his hand from mine, correctly reading that I want to have this moment with my mom.

As Derek steps back, my mom takes his place. She leans over the bed and gathers me in her arms.

I breathe her in and a hundred memories from my childhood flare to life in my mind. It's as if a self-protective dam has broken and her presence called the memories to life. The two of us baking bread in the warm kitchen of my childhood home. Volunteering and singing Christmas carols at the nursing home in town. Taking long walks in the summer and picking wildflowers to display in the blue vase on the kitchen table.

"Thank God you're okay," she murmurs in my hair.

"Thank you for coming."

"Oh, Allegra," she murmurs, her voice cracking. "I'm so sorry I stayed away for so long. I used to ask God to forgive me." She pulls back and cups my cheek. Her eyes meet mine. "But now, now I just want your forgiveness. Could you try to give it to me? Even if I'm not worthy of it."

"Mom," I sob, holding out my arm.

She hugs me again. Over her shoulder, I note the tears that fall down Levi's cheeks. The emotion that swells in Derek's expression as he stuffs his hands in his pockets and looks away.

I manage a deep inhale and even though it sets the side of my body on fire, another old wound, scabbed over but so deep it aches, begins to heal.

"You're here now," I say. "That's what matters."

THAT AFTERNOON, before I'm discharged, Derek and Levi skip out for coffee and give me a chance to catch up with Mom.

"Levi called," she admits from the chair beside my bed.

"He did?" Wow. For Levi to reach out to Mom after years of being estranged is huge.

Did he do it for me?

I recall my past few weeks with Levi; the guy he's become since he left rehab. I think he knows, deep down, it's what I still want. A relationship with our parents, a way home so to speak.

Mom nods, dabbing at tears in the corners of her eyes. "My heart was in my toes. I was petrified. Panicked. And then, he offered to fly me out. I heard myself saying yes. I hung up, packed a bag, left your father a note, and...I'm here."

"You left Dad a note?" I can't hide the disbelief from my tone.

Mom sputters a laugh, but it's edged with nerves. "I did. I wasn't thinking clearly."

"Have you heard from him?"

"He's not happy," she admits. "But neither was I. Not since you left." Mom leans forward again and recaptures my hand. "I'm sorry, Allegra. When you went away to college, I kept praying you'd find your way home. It was always the way I defined home. The Church, the community, marriage, and family. But when Levi called and my heart dropped, I realized maybe you are home. You and Levi." She smiles sadly. "You have a community here with your social justice outreach and your friends. Levi told me you and Derek are together. That he hasn't left your side in weeks." She shakes her head. "Even the way he protected you when I knocked on the door... You have a man who loves you. A brother who wants to be with you. A waiting room filled with people, true friends, who care about you." A tear spills onto her cheek. "Deep down, you have more of a home than I do. And I'm sorry."

"Mom," I whisper, gripping her hand. The regret in her tone breaks my heart because I know she means it. We haven't had the relationship I wanted in years, maybe even ever, but I never gave up hope that one day, we'd connect. Deep down, I always sensed that if she could shake off my father's thumb, she'd embrace me for who I am. Her daughter.

"No," she refutes. "Don't feel bad for me. I made the choices I did and now, I must live with them."

"I'd like for us to have a relationship again," I murmur. "I want you to know my friends, Derek, my life here in LA."

Surprise rings her irises. "Really?" Hesitant hope weaves through her voice.

"Really. I love my life here. It's my home now. But I miss you. I love you. I want you in my life too," I clarify. If this past year has taught me anything, it's the power of forgiveness. It's knowing people can change. It's believing in second chances. Just like Dex encouraged me to.

"Oh, Allegra." Her face falls again. "I want you in my life, too. I never, not for a second, stopped loving you, sweet girl."

"And Dad?" I hate the hope that sparks in my words.

"If your father continues to miss out, then that's his choice. And he'll have to live with it." I've never heard her speak so harshly about my father before.

Her words ease some of the rejection I've felt from my father. I know she's been on the receiving end of his disapproval. Has she felt the same dejection? Has she sought out his love and acceptance like me? If she's managed to come to terms with it, after sharing more than half of her life with him, why can't I?

I squeeze my mom's hand. In doing so, some of the bitterness I harbor toward my father fades. He doesn't deserve to take up space in either of our thoughts. "Let's go home."

Mom smiles.

Ten minutes later, Derek and Levi reappear. Dr. Reese discharges me from the hospital.

"How do you feel about shacking up with me?" Derek murmurs as he helps me into a wheelchair.

"What?" I ask, my eyes darting to my mother. Behind her, I note Levi watching me curiously.

I glance back to Derek.

"He wants some time with her," Derek explains, tipping his head toward Levi. "Something about making amends..."

"Oh. Yeah, um, okay," I agree.

Derek snorts. "You could sound a little more enthusiastic, Stellina. I've been tasked with giving you a sponge bath." He winks.

I groan.

He grins.

As Derek wheels me toward the parking lot, I check my messages. With the commotion of Mom arriving, my friends texted their well wishes, promising to drop by to see me during the week.

Nova: I'm getting ice cream delivered to your place.

Ivy: Ice cream? Our girl needs wine.

Kenny: Are you really okay, A? We've been so worried.

Nova: Girl, your mom showing up...PLOT. TWIST.

Ivy: How's that going?

Kenny: Is she staying in town for a while?

Ivy: Levi was so sweet when he brought her up. He was ushering her forward and had this look on his face...totally astonished.

Kenny: He just seemed really happy to see her, you know?

Nova: Derek didn't give a fuckkkkk. He wouldn't leave

your room UNTIL your mama showed up and Levi made him.

Me: How do you girls know all this?

Nova: Maverick. Duh.

Ivy: He's got all the tea.

Kenny: Yeah, he spills it too. (eye roll emoji)

Me: You girls are the best! Thank you for spending so much time in the waiting room, waiting for me.

Ivy: What else is new? (sarcastic face emoji)

Kenny: Of course!

Nova: Are you home??

Me: Well, another plot twist...with mom being in town and Levi also wanting some time with her (of course)...I'm staying at Derek's.

Nova: YOU MOVED IN!

Ivy: I knew this would happen.

Kenny: Are you sure about this? You can stay with us too...

Nova: Yeah, Ivy'll wear her nurse costume from Halloween last year if you want! Tell Reign we can make shit official too.

Ivy: HA!

Kenny: I'm serious, A. You have options.

Me: I know. AND THANK YOU. But I'm good with it. He's been by my side since everything went down and has been taking great care of me. I'm feeling better already.

Kenny: How bad was it?

Me: Scary. Scary as shit. But I'm okay.

Ivy: Levi wanted to go nuclear.

Nova: Derek too. Mav was the voice of reason.

Ivy: Yeah, he called your bank and had your credit cards cancelled.

Kenny: Maverick Tate is never a voice of reason.

Nova: Just because he gets under your skin doesn't mean he isn't the most entertaining guy in any room.

Ivy: Fact.

Kenny: Whatever. Allegra, we're sending ice cream and wine to Derek's.

Nova: Oh yeah! Doing that now.

Ivy: LOVE YOU.

Kenny: We'll come by this week.

Me: Can't wait! I miss you.

Kenny: Get rest! (heart emoji)

Nova: Get D! (eggplant emoji)

Ivy: (sarcastic face emoji, laughing face emoji, kissing face emoji)

Kenny: I don't know what's happening anymore.

I laugh at my friends' messages. Derek opens the passenger car door and stares at me, his gaze questioning.

"The girls." I shake my phone before dropping it beside me. "Don't be surprised if a delivery arrives."

Derek's lips curl into a smile on one side. "They were worried about you." He helps me into the car and carefully clips in my seat belt, folding up a hoodie so the strap doesn't cut into my ribs.

"Yeah," I say shakily, breathing through the discomfort of moving my body.

"We all were."

"I know," I say quietly. "It was terrifying."

"Christ, Stellina." Derek dips down to press a kiss to the crown of my head. "Let's go home, baby."

"Yeah," I agree.

But when Derek pulls back, his eyes are still questioning. There's a glimmer of unease that puts me on alert.

He slides into the driver seat and takes us to his condo. We ride in silence, each of us lost in our thoughts.

What has Derek on edge? Is it the attack? The future?

How are things unfolding between Mom and Levi? Is he making amends? Are they forgiving each other? Is it awkward? Will she stay in town long?

Should I postpone my interviews? Can I interview virtually, over Zoom? Or on the phone?

When we arrive at Derek's, I don't have answers to any of my questions and I'm too tired to sort them out. Derek helps me into his condo and settles me into his king-sized bed. I relax against the pillows as the doorbell rings.

"I'll get it," Derek says, moving toward the front door. Before he exits, he glances at me. "You okay?"

I smile. "Yes. Answer the door."

He appears a moment later, holding up a care package.

I chuckle when I see the postcard of *Magic Mike*.

"What the hell is this?" He sneers, turning it over. He reads it aloud. "Get that D, girl! It'll make you feel better. Love, us."

Derek looks at me. I dissolve into laughter before I wince, holding my ribs.

"Be careful, beauty," he warns.

"What else did they send?" I ask.

Derek places the box down on his bed and I open it up.

"Ice cream," I say, pulling out the mini-freezer inside. It's stocked with several delicious flavors.

"Birthday cake?" Derek questions.

"It's the best!" I pull out a bottle of wine and one of champagne.

"Damn," Derek laughs.

"A code for *Magic Mike*." I roll my eyes, dropping the slip of paper with the download information on it.

Derek shakes his head, but his eyes are lit up with amusement instead of uncertainty. I relax slightly.

I unpack the remainder of snacks and look at Derek. "Got plans today?"

"Just you," he replies.

I gesture to the supplies on his bed. "Wine, junk food, and a movie?"

"We're watching *Magic Mike*, aren't we?" he groans.

I smile. "We're totally watching *Magic Mike*."

Derek sighs. He goes to the kitchen to stock the ice cream but returns a moment later with a tray holding two bowls of birthday cake ice cream, two wine glasses, and some napkins. He slips into the bed beside me.

We download the movie, lean back, and hang out.

We watch *Magic Mike*, eat ice cream in bed, and howl with laughter. Well, I laugh as much as I'm capable of. It's really Derek's reactions to the film that fill me with amusement.

Afterwards, Derek kisses me sweetly and puts me to bed.

And I feel like I'm home. The one Mom talked about.

TWENTY-ONE

DEREK

THAT NIGHT, Allegra and I have dinner with Levi and her mom at our place. I've insisted she refer to the condo as her home too. It's taking her time to warm up to that idea, which is why my thoughts keep circling back to a house. Mine and hers.

It's a nice, civil dinner filled with polite conversation and a tentative acceptance that everyone wants to move forward but no one knows how to take the first step without rocking the boat.

In the past, I would've dropped a fucking bomb in the center of it and ruined dinner enough to be a distraction.

But tonight, I'm quiet. Every time I look at Allegra's bruised face and split lip, I feel nauseous. The warnings Dex, Mav, and Allegra all implied about my rushing things flicker at the edges of my mind.

I feel helpless. Stuck. Restless and anxious and so damn frustrated.

Someone put his hands on my girl, and I wasn't there to stop it. Months ago, she was numbing her heartache with drugs and other fucking men, and I had no goddamn clue.

Fuck, we made a baby together and I was too messed up for her to trust me with the information.

How many times am I going to fail her? How many times am I going to come up short?

Why won't she take the next step with me? Does she not trust me to keep her safe? Does she not love me with the same all-consuming desire I have for her?

Or is she truly happy with the way things are? She keeps saying she is but...

There's no certainty. There's no plan.

Is she going to keep working downtown? Will she continue to put herself at risk? What if this happens again? What if, no matter how hard I fucking try, I can't protect her?

That's the bitterest pill to swallow. What if she gets hurt, again? What if I can't stop it? What if I'm not enough for her?

I couldn't help my mom and look how that turned out. She was dead before her forty-fifth birthday.

After a stifled dessert and coffee, Levi and his mom stand to leave. We say good night at the door. I manage to hug Allegra's mom good-bye and when I pull away, she gives me a long, searching look.

"What?" I whisper, caught off guard by her blatant study of me. While Mrs. Rousell and I have exchanged conversation in the past, no one knows about it. It's only because I recognized, deep down, that she loves her children relentlessly. The way a mother is supposed to. The way my mother didn't. And because of that, I let her know that I'd watch out for Levi when he moved to Boston.

And I fucking let him down too, didn't I?

She smiles. "You're good for her."

I chuckle. "No, I'm not."

"You are," she counters. "I had to see it to believe it. Now, you need to believe it, too."

She turns back to Levi and the two of them make their way down the hall. My friend lifts his hand in farewell. Allegra steps next to me, and I slip my arm around her shoulders.

We stand in the doorway and watch them enter the elevator before going back inside.

"Well, that was kind of awkward," Allegra comments.

"It was a good first step. It'll take time," I reassure her.

"Yeah. I'm happy she's here."

"Has your dad reached out?" I ask.

She shakes her head. "He's furious with my mom. So much so…I don't know what will happen." A streak of pain ripples across her face.

"What is it? Your ribs?" I'm at her side in a second, helping her toward the couch and easing her down. "Want some ibuprofen?"

"No." She shakes her head. "No, I was just wondering if my parents would get divorced."

"Oh." I sit down on the coffee table in front of her. I had to buy a new, sturdier one. "Would that be so bad?"

She snorts. It's a sound of choked laugher and disbelief. "I can't imagine it. I mean, they would be shunned from their community. From the only world they know."

"Maybe they would find a better, more accepting, community."

Allegra shakes her head. "Not everyone is like you. You adapt easily. Go with the flow."

"Roll with the punches," I correct her. "It's survival."

"I guess. I just, I'm worried about my mom."

I reach for her hand. Play with her fingers. "I know. But she's here."

"Yeah." She smiles. "She's here."

"Is she planning on staying?" I delve into new territory.

"She has to go back eventually." Allegra pauses and bites her bottom lip. "She asked Levi and me if we have to plans to ever come back home."

I sit up straighter. "To live?"

Allegra shrugs.

"Do you?" I press.

What if she doesn't stay in LA? Would she move to Boston? Or the small town in Massachusetts she grew up in?

"I, I don't know."

"Allegra," I clear my throat. "I know you're waiting to hear back about interviews and potential job offers but long term...baby, what's your plan? Where do you see yourself? See us?" I throw it all out.

Annoyance flickers across her expression. "I don't know. I'm still waiting to hear back from the Harrison Foundation. They're unrolling some new programs here, in LA. In the meantime, I want to continue my work at the NGO and—"

"You're serious?" I interrupt her. Bite my fucking tongue the second the words are out of my mouth.

She rears back. "Yes. Why?"

"Stellina, look at you." I gesture toward her body. Bruised face. Cracked fucking ribs.

She glares at me and I'm so relieved to see that she still has her fire, that spark I love, that I relax slightly. "Don't like what you see, Derek?"

I laugh. "I fucking love what I see. I love everything about you. But, baby, what if something like this happens again?"

She softens slightly. "Derek, this could've happened anywhere."

"No." I shake my head. "Your odds are greater working in that area, where a lot of homeless—"

"The man who did this was high."

"I know."

"He could've been suffering from a mental-health issue."

"He could've," I agree.

She frowns. "I'm not going to stop doing work I love because of one incident. It was a fluke."

"You think this was a fluke? Allegra, if you hadn't been in a desolate area, at night, by yourself, do you think—"

"Yes!" she cuts me off. "I think I could've been in the middle of a mall in broad daylight and a person struggling with addiction or mental health could've robbed me."

"Fuck," I swear, turning away. Glance back at her. "What if you had been pregnant, Allegra? What if—"

"Don't," she bites out. A warning.

"I'm just saying—"

"I know what you're saying." She struggles to stand.

I move closer to help her, but she swats my hand away.

"Do you want a family with me? Do you trust me enough for that?" The words come out of my mouth on a broken whisper. I didn't mean to speak them. I wish I hadn't said them.

But they're out. Humming in the space between us.

Anguish twists my beauty's face. "Derek." She reaches for me.

This time, I step away.

"I wasn't there to protect you," I tell her.

Confusion swirls in her irises. "You weren't supposed to be. You can't always—"

"What if you'd been pregnant, Allegra? What if I lost you? Our baby. What if—"

"You can't live in what-ifs, Derek," she says. "You know that."

"I don't want you to work there." My voice is forged in steel.

Allegra chuckles, the sound a mixture of sarcasm and disbelief. "Well, too fucking bad. I'm not giving up my career aspirations because of this." She points to her bandaged ribs.

"I'm not asking you to give up anything. I'm asking you to think things through. To consider the dangers. The unpredictability of it."

"Life is unpredictable, Derek."

"I need you to be safe," I mutter. "I need *you*."

"I need you, too. I need your support." She steps toward me. "Can't we just see how things play out?"

I shrug. "Fine. Let's say you get a job here and take it. Then what? You want to stay two years, five years, ten? Do you want to—"

"I want what I've always wanted," she cuts me off. Her voice is quiet. Her eyes are sad, her mouth beautiful.

I shift my weight from one foot to the next, waiting for her words.

"You. A family, a future, a life, with you, Derek. But not at the expense of me." She sighs. "I'm tired. I'm going to bed. Good night."

With that, she walks into our bedroom and closes the door.

"Fuck," I swear at the empty room. Energy still rolls through my veins. I'm antsy, on edge. Nothing has been resolved. There's still no certainty. Still no goddamn plan.

Wait. See. Let it unfold. Decide once things pan out.

How am I supposed to know what to do based on variables? A hundred hypotheticals with no plan on how to manage any of them?

I stand in silence for a few moments, replaying our conversation.

I could've handled that better. I should've handled that better.

I bombarded her with my own insecurities after she confessed her concern over her mom.

Now, she's pissed off, and I'm more twisted up than I was at dinner.

I retreat to the kitchen and clean up.

Then, I grab my keys and wallet and head out.

I plan to take a walk. Instead, I dial Dex and ask him to meet for a burger.

TWENTY-TWO
ALLEGRA

I WINCE when I hear the front door close. Tears pool in the corners of my eyes, but I blink them away.

Sinking to the edge of the mattress, I lean back into the propped pillows at the head of the bed.

My mom sacrificed her whole life, all her dreams, for my father and the life he wanted. She wasn't permitted to hold a job or earn her own money, even after Levi and I were in school.

She was dutiful and obedient and a loving mother, but my father's word always held more weight.

Now, look at her. Trying to re-establish a connection with her grown children after missing out on our lives for the past four-plus years.

I love my work. I love the purpose it gives me and the impact it makes on a community I care about.

My hand cups my lower abdomen.

And I loved—love—my fruit slice. I would like to be a mother one day. I'd cherish the opportunity to grow a family.

Why can't I do both?

Why can't Derek see that we can have both? Support each other through it all?

Picking up my phone, I tap out a message to the group thread.

Me: Derek left.

Nova: Again?

Ivy: Left...how?

Kenny: Want us to come over?

My phone buzzes a moment later.

I snort when I click accept on the Group FaceTime.

"What do you mean he left?" Nova dives right in.

"Is he drunk?" Ivy asks.

"Angry?" Kenny guesses.

I sigh again. "We got into an argument. A disagreement."

"About?" Mckenna raises her eyebrows.

"He thinks my work at the NGO is too dangerous. He wants to know if I'm planning to stay in LA or head back to Massachusetts. Or I guess just what my plans are in general."

"Okay," Ivy says slowly.

"The NGO is kind of dangerous," Nova says. "I mean, you broke two ribs, A."

"That was a one-off thing," I remind her.

"You sure?" Ivy asks gently.

"You guys! This is the career I want," I push back.

"True," Ivy says. "And you worked hard for it. But Derek being worried, even if you don't want him to be, doesn't make him a dick."

"And him wanting to know where your head's at for the future isn't that weird either," Mckenna admits.

"Ugh. It's like everyone wants to know what our life

plans are now that we graduated," Nova laments. "Can't a girl take a minute? Enjoy a hot girl summer?"

"Exactly!" I exclaim, pointing at Nova. "Why do I have to have it all figured out?" I wince as I twist my body toward the camera.

Nova points back, her eyes narrowed in concern. "Dangerous."

I sigh.

"You don't have to have it all figured out, babe," Ivy says slowly. "It sounds like Derek is just grappling. He probably feels like he let you down."

"He said he feels like he didn't protect me," I admit.

"I get why he'd feel that way," Mckenna offers. "It may explain why he's been all up in your business lately, too. I know you feel like he's trying to make decisions for you, which is a nonstarter, but I think he's only doing that because he's worried."

"He is." I groan, exhaling my frustration. "But it's annoying."

Nova snickers. "Who thought Derek would end up being the clingy one?"

"Not me." Mckenna shakes her head.

I roll my eyes.

"Derek's not exactly a 'let's-talk-about-our-feelings' kind of guy," Nova says. "The only way he knows how to show you how he feels is by exerting control. Making the decisions. Taking action."

"Did he pack a bag?" Mckenna asks. "When he left?"

"What? No." I shake my head.

"So, he's like...out blowing off steam?" Ivy wonders.

"I guess. I just, I don't know what he wants me to say. I love my work. I'm not going to quit because of this one thing that happened," I defend my point.

"Fair," Mckenna agrees.

"Is he asking you to quit?" Nova asks. "Or is he asking you to let him know what's up and what you're thinking because he's worried about you?"

"You scared the shit out of all of us, but Derek..." Ivy trails off.

"He nearly fought an EMT when he came into the hospital," Mckenna recalls.

"I don't want to sacrifice my dreams and give things up for a guy. Not even Derek," I refute their points.

"You shouldn't," Nova says encouragingly.

"But is that what Derek's asking you to do?" Ivy asks.

I roll my neck. Crack it. "No."

Mckenna chuckles. "I'm so glad it was just a disagreement."

"Yeah. He'll be back in a bit, ready to make up," Ivy agrees.

Nova waggles her eyebrows. "We all know what that means."

"An apology," Mckenna supplies.

Nova groans. "Hot sex, Kenny. Jeez, you gotta get laid."

Mckenna blushes. Ivy laughs.

I grin. "So you think everything's okay?"

"If you're asking if I think he actually bolted, it's all good. But you gotta see where he's coming from, A. It's been easy to hate on Derek because he fucked up so many times but this boy, he's trying now. He's doing his best and while his bossy methods aren't ideal, they're coming from a place of concern," Nova dishes out.

"He loves you," Ivy says simply.

"And he made some good points." Mckenna's always the rational friend.

"Enjoy the D," Nova says dreamily.

"Like your football player isn't throwing down," Ivy claps back.

"We can hear you!" Mckenna supplies.

I laugh again. "Okay. Thank you. I feel better."

"Good." Mckenna smiles.

"Brunch tomorrow?" Ivy asks.

"Our spot at ten," Nova confirms. She looks at me. "Are you feeling up to it? If not, we can come to you and—"

"I'll be there," I promise. While I'm not fully recovered, I'm healing, and seeing my friends will cheer me up.

"See you tomorrow," Mckenna tells the group.

"Night!" I disconnect the call.

Then, I turn on the television and watch a match-making show while I wait for Derek to return home.

"ALLEGRA." He appears in the bedroom doorway an hour and a half later.

Apology and regret are stamped in his expression. I sit up straighter in bed and flip off the television.

He strides to my bedside. His presence fills the room, his cologne washes over me, and my body lights up, in tune to his intensity, and ready for his touch.

I open my arms and he sinks into them, perching on the edge of the mattress. Derek's body covers mine and I breathe him in as he kisses my cheek.

"I'm sorry," I say.

"I'm fucking sorry," he replies.

I chuckle. Derek pulls back and grins at me.

"I don't want to fight with you," he swears.

"That was a disagreement," I correct him.

"I don't even want to do that."

"It's healthy sometimes."

"Maybe. But tonight, fuck, I hate how I felt. I don't like not knowing what's next for us. And I know you have a lot going on. There are things to think about, things to process. But, Stellina, I'm here. I'm all in with you. So much so that I can't think about anything else. I can't plan or hope or dream. I can't even fucking breathe half the time. If you don't want this, the future, the family, you need to tell me. You need to tell me to leave, or you need to walk away. Because it won't be me."

"I don't want you to go. And I don't want to leave. I want the future and the family and all of it. I also want a career that I love," I explain myself.

"I know you love your job. I know social justice issues are important to you and it's something I fucking admire. It's something that drew me to you when you first showed up at the brownstone." He tucks my hair behind my ear. "You impress me all the damn time. But lately, after the baby, after this"—he glances at my ribs—"I'm half panicked all the fucking time. My thoughts are twisted, and I can't think straight."

"Because you care about me."

"Because I love you more than life." His hand palms my cheek and I lift my hand to hold his touch against my skin.

"I love you too," I whisper, hearing his truths. Understanding, maybe for the first time, that I'm not the only one who truly suffered from the loss we experienced. Derek's been better at concealing his pain, but I should have taken his worries more seriously. I should have tried harder to understand his concerns. "And I hear you about the NGO. I understand where you're coming from. I promise to think things through, okay? I need you to trust me. Trust my decisions and my ability to make them for myself."

"Okay," he breathes out. His eyes flash with a reluctant glare but his lips curl slightly in a smile.

"It's hard for you, isn't it?" I tease.

"What?"

"To give in to me."

He chuckles and shifts his body over mine. "No, baby. Giving in to you is fucking easy. Resisting you is the hard part." He kisses the corner of my mouth, away from my stitches.

"Right now, I want to stay in LA and be with you. I want us to do work that we love, that fills our souls and creative cups. I want time with you, Derek. Moments and magic." My eyes meet his and I fall forward, into their bottomless depths.

He places a hand on my hip and leans closer. "I want you, Stellina. I'll live wherever you want. I just want to know your thoughts, your desires, your wishes. I want you to trust me and I want in on your plans. I want to take care of you. And protect you. And provide for you. I want you to be happy and healthy and safe. And I want to love you every fucking day of my life, and even afterwards. Forever."

His words wash over me. They're the most open and vulnerable he's ever been, and I wrap myself in the assurances they provide.

"I do trust you," I say, meaning it fully. "And I want all of that too."

Derek smiles. "Good. Then we're on the same page."

"Yes," I breathe out.

Derek brushes a kiss to the center of my forehead.

I give him a hug. "Where'd you go?"

He pulls back. "Had a burger with my dad."

I laugh, happy to hear it. "You and Dex really clicked, huh?"

"He's a laid-back guy. Makes it easy for me."

"I never heard you call him dad before," I say gently.

Derek nods. "I never thought we'd have dinner with your mom, as a couple."

"True," I agree. "We're really making strides with our families."

He takes my hand in his and rests our joined fingers on my stomach.

"Yeah. I think I'm more open to it now, that...well, the baby brought our family together," Derek says softly.

"You really want to have children with me?" I ask, my voice catching. Vulnerability rises to the surface as I think of our little fruit, of the risks that future pregnancies may hold.

"More than you know." He kisses the corner of my mouth again. "But there's no rush, Stellina. We have our whole future ahead of us."

"We do, Derek," I agree, smiling sheepishly. "We can start house hunting now."

My rockstar gives me the biggest grin and I laugh, lunging forward to kiss him again.

"I LIKE IT," Maverick states, unprompted.

"This is it, isn't it?" I agree, glancing up at the home. Over the past month, Allegra and I have driven through areas of LA, pointing out houses we like, noting restaurants and coffee bars and parks. We've looked into nursery schools and doctors' offices, gyms and swimming pools.

And my girl keeps coming back to this property. This home. There's something in her expression that softens when she takes in the Spanish-styled stucco home with the red tiled roof and big windows. It's historic and vintage.

The first time we drove by, a small sigh dropped from her mouth. A smile curved her lips. And I haven't seen that expression cross her face since.

Deep down, I know this is the home of her heart.

While we aren't rushing into anything, we've started planning for our future. Knowing that we're on the same page, coupled with Allegra's taking an active interest in our next chapter in LA, has eased my nerves.

While she started her road to recovery, she also embarked on a slew of job interviews with various NGOs and outreach programs in the greater LA area. On the nights that she works at the NGO, I pick her up and take her home. We sit down to a dinner I made, like a real family, and share parts of our day.

When she has plans with her girls, I hang out with Levi, Mav, and Jameson.

When she goes out for a coffee or shopping with her mom, I hit Dex up.

Each week, the future I've dreamed about becomes more of a reality.

Now, I think Allegra is ready to take the next step. And, if I'm being honest, I don't want us to miss out on this house, since I know she loves it.

My eyes sweep over the home. It's hardly contemporary. Or flashy. There's no state-of-the-art outdoor kitchen or expansive lawn.

But it's gorgeous in a well-loved kind of way.

"It's her." Dex nods beside me.

"Plus, she loves this area," Levi says, glancing around the street. It's just off the beaten path. Close to the restaurants and coffee shops Allegra frequents with her friends.

"It's a good choice," Jameson weighs in.

I glance at him. Out of my circle, he knows Allegra the least, yet he states the words with confidence.

At my look, he continues, "She wouldn't want something she couldn't put her own touch on. And a new, contemporary, pristine home wouldn't lend that type of warmth. Allegra likes to leave a mark. I mean," he laughs lightly, "look at us."

The guys and I—my bandmates, my best friends, my fucking dad—glance at each other before cracking up.

"True story, mate." I smack Jameson on the back.

Deb comes out of the house and meets us in the backyard. Her sixties-inspired bouffant hairstyle doesn't move in the breeze. "So..." She beams. "What do you think?"

"I'll take it," I say, stepping to Deb to put in an offer.

The guys hang back, talking about the house, shooting the shit, just relaxing. I snap a quick photo of the home and send it to Dre.

Me: (photo attached) What do you think?

Dre: Looks like home.

I snort because, of course, Dre gets it. Gets me.

Me: You gotta get out here.

Dre: Throw a housewarming party. I'll roll through.

I laugh again because Dre knows I'd never throw a fucking housewarming. But I'll convince him to roll through anyway. Entering the house behind Deb, we relocate to the kitchen, and I put in an offer I know the current owners will accept.

I buy the type of home I always yearned for as a kid. The home that makes my Stellina smile.

"Pleasure doing business with you, Derek." Deb shakes my hand.

"Thanks, Deb."

She grins. "Welcome home."

I look around the space. The kitchen flows into a living room and wraps into an all-seasons enclosed porch.

I can see Allegra sitting there, reading. I can envision our future children playing blocks or chasing each other around the backyard. I can see Dre flipping me shit while manning the grill. And Levi giving his sister a hard time while Mav lounges in a floatie in the pool, a beer in hand, and Jameson kicks back, taking it all in.

Dex mixing drinks. Allegra's mom with a grandkid on her hip.

And me, smiling at my Stellina like she makes my world go round. Because she does.

I can see it all.

Fucking magic.

THE FOLLOWING WEEK, I close on the property and Allegra is cleared by Dr. Reese to increase her physical activity.

"Does this mean we can do it again?" I murmur, kissing the back of her head, as I wrap my arms around her.

She laughs, turning her head. I kiss her cheek.

"Yes," she whispers, dancing out of my grasp. "Tonight," she promises.

I groan. "Why not now?"

"We're heading to Beirut for lunch," she explains.

"We are?" I raise an eyebrow, pretending I don't know this afternoon's plan when I'm the one who set it in motion.

"Yes. My mom has decided to stay in LA for a while. Dex has kindly offered the help of his lawyer to help Mom navigate the landmines of separating from my father."

"Shit," I whisper. I didn't realize Dex was going to spin such a tale to convince Allegra to swing by Beirut. Dex mentioned a few times that he's worried about Mrs. Rousell, but I also didn't think he was actively engaged in helping her.

Allegra faces me and scrunches her nose. "I know. But I think this is good for her."

"She looks a lot better now than when she arrived," I comment.

Allegra swats my stomach. "Derek!"

"What? She does. She looks happier. Laughs more too."

Allegra is thoughtful for a moment. "She does laugh more."

I lift an eyebrow as if to say, *see, I'm right.*

Allegra grins. "Want to come to lunch?"

I stifle my chuckle at her invitation. Sweet Stellina, if only she knew what I have in store for her. "Sure. I want to show you something too. Can we take a detour on the way to Beirut?"

Allegra glances at the time. "If we leave now."

I chuckle. My girl is always fucking punctual. I tug on her hand. "Let's go."

"YOU READY FOR YOUR SURPRISE?" I ask as we near the home.

"What?" She glances at me. "What surprise?"

I park the car. "For graduation, Stellina."

"You didn't have to get me anything."

I roll my eyes and round the car to open her door. Extending my hand, I beckon for her to exit. "Come on."

She stands and, lacing her hand with mine, falls into step beside me.

"I love this area," she comments, her tone wistful.

My heartbeat races and I roll my lips together to hold back my laughter, to conceal my excitement.

Together, we approach her new home. I reach into my pocket and pull out a key. Then, I raise our joined hands, slip my fingers from hers, and place the key in her open palm.

"Welcome home, Stellina. I hope all your dreams come true."

She stares at me in awe. Shock blooms in her expression as her gaze darts from my face to the house and back again.

"You...bought this house?" she asks slowly. "The house I love?"

I smile and dip my head. "It's yours. The deed's in your name."

She gasps. "What?"

"It's a graduation present," I explain.

"It's too much," she refutes.

I laugh. She's too fucking much. "It's not nearly enough. I'm in this with you, Allegra. I've said it over and over. I've tried like hell to fucking prove it. But I want you to know, without a shadow of a doubt, that I'm yours. I'm here. I'm happy. I fucking love you. Please, let me live here with you and keep making plans for our future?"

"Derek!" She gapes. "I can't, this is..." She stares at the key in her palm. "I don't know what to say."

"Say you want this as much as I do," I murmur the words. They're hopeful as fuck and I hate how vulnerable I sound. How raw I feel. But for her, I'll lay my shit bare.

Her expression softens and her eyes clear. They hold mine, deep and tender. Filled with emotion. "I want everything you want and more."

She closes the space between us and winds her arms around my neck. "I love you," she says simply. "Always have." Then, she kisses me, and I see stars.

I carefully sweep my girl up into my arms and walk toward the front of the house. I keep my hold on Allegra until I maneuver opening the door and step across the threshold.

She giggles. "You're supposed to do that on our wedding night."

"I'll do it then too," I promise. I set her on her feet and flip on the light.

Allegra sighs dreamily and my heart nearly bursts. I watch every emotion flit across her face.

Awe. Excitement. Disbelief. Happiness. Love.

So much fucking love I could drown in it.

And never come up for air.

She turns toward me, her hands clasped beneath her chin. "Thank you, Derek."

"Don't thank me, Stellina." I take her hand in mine. "Just, do this with me."

"I already am," she murmurs. Then, she tugs on my hand and drags me from one room to the next.

I love the sounds of pleasure that fall from her mouth when she discovers something she likes.

"A walk-in closet! This is wild!"

And then, "This would be a perfect nursery."

"Oh my God! Did you know it's been a long-held dream of mine to have a window seat?"

"Could I have a library?"

Or... "A gazebo! We need a gazebo!"

I follow along, beaming from ear to ear and saying yes to everything she wants. I want to give her the fucking world since she's mine. My whole entire reason for being happy is wrapped up in her perfect curves and big, brown eyes.

I'm such a lucky bastard, I can barely process it.

"Come here." Allegra beckons me closer when I enter the master bedroom.

I lift an eyebrow. "You want to christen it now?"

I expect her laughter. I'm ready for her to shove me playfully in the stomach.

I'm one-hundred percent not prepared for my girl to

shimmy out of her sundress. It slides down her body like silk and pools around her feet. She steps out of it, neat and prim, like she's doing a fucking party trick and not blowing my mind.

"Now?" I sputter, glancing at my watch like it matters. Time stands still when I'm with Allegra and everything in my world, save for her, disappears.

She unhooks her strapless bra and drops it on the floor in response.

Her ribs still show fading bruises. They break my fucking heart, but the love shimmering in her gaze is powerful enough to distract me from what happened.

"Right now," she murmurs, her voice husky. Throaty. Needy.

"Fuck, baby," I reply, losing my shirt.

Allegra reaches for the waistband of my pants and opens the button, drags down the fly, and pushes my jeans off my hips. I kick them off as she drags my boxer briefs down my legs.

Before I can process what's happening, she's on her knees. My cock twitches against her mouth and her eyes—those warm, chocolate, begging eyes—find mine.

"Jesus," I breathe out.

Allegra smirks. Sassy and saucy and fucking hot as hell. She guides me into her mouth and doesn't stop until I hit the back of her throat.

"Allegra," I moan. My palm slides over her head, my fingers tangling in her hair.

Her grip on my base tightens and she begins to bob her head. Her mouth and hand work in tandem, driving me to the edge a lot faster than I want. My body tingles and tightens as I drink in the visual of her, before me, on her knees...shit.

"Fuck, slow down," I sputter. "It's been a minute," I remind her.

She releases my cock with a pop and grins at me. "Gotta work on your stamina, Reign," she teases, gently squeezing my balls.

I bark out a laugh that's half delirious and pull her up. Palm her ass and lift her. "Smart ass," I murmur, turning to pin her against the wall.

My mouth crashes over hers. Our kiss is passionate, our hands tracking and tracing each other's bodies. I grind my erection against her core, and she mewls, giving me those sounds I love. They should be on a fucking album, but I'd never let anyone else hear her.

Not like this. Not when she's mine.

I cup her, loving how her heat spreads through the silk of her panties.

"Need you," she pleads.

I lay her out, right in the middle of the empty fucking master bedroom.

Her hair fans around her head like a halo. A goddamn angel.

I snap her panties at the hip and fist the material in my hand.

"Derek," she gasps. "I can't wear a dress with no underwear."

I laugh. "Wanna bet?" I travel down her body until I can kiss her right there. She bucks against my mouth and I palm her thigh, holding in her place while I drag my tongue up her core.

"Oh God," she moans.

My hand snakes up her body to play with her nipple as I lap at her, sucking gently on her clit.

"Derek," she pants. "Need you."

I play for a few more minutes until she's writhing against my mouth. Then, I line myself up at her entrance and push inside. Her eyes widen and a moan—guttural, raw, needy—fills the air.

"Goddamn, beauty," I swear as I bottom out.

I fall forward and brace one hand next to her head as I begin to move. Our pace is steady. A series of sharp thrusts followed by long and smooth. I work my girl up until she cries out, her pussy pulsing around my cock.

I drag out her orgasm for as long as I can, kissing her neck and pinching her nipples. Only then, when her hazy eyes meet mine, do I find my release.

I come hard. Fast. My vision blurs as emotion I've never experienced swells and crests. I break apart. Unravel.

"Holy shit," I swear, dropping on top of Allegra.

I gather her in my arms and roll to the side, holding her against my chest.

She giggles. She fucking giggles and presses a kiss to my pec.

"Welcome home, Derek," she whispers.

I look at her, note the lightness in her eyes, the grin that curls her mouth. Drink in her pure perfection.

Then, I laugh. I crack up until tears fill my eyes and my stomach hurts.

I hold on to my beauty who laughs with me. The two of us live in this magical moment knowing it's only the beginning.

TWENTY-FOUR
ALLEGRA

LEVI: *Are you on your way?*

Dex: Hey, A! The lawyer just got here. You still coming?

Mom: Allegra, is everything okay? I thought you'd be here by now...

I sputter when I read the messages. Derek glances at my phone over my shoulder as he ties the back of my dress. He laughs and kisses the back of my neck. "Don't worry, baby. I'll drive fast."

"Great," I deadpan at his terrible solution.

He chuckles and heads for the stairs. I take a moment to glance around the master bedroom. I can't believe Derek bought us—me—a house. I can't believe we're really taking the next step together.

If someone told me a year ago that I'd be moving in with Derek Reiner, as his significant other, I'd tell them they were spinning tall tales. But here we are, making my dreams a reality.

I shake my head. It almost feels too good to be true.

"Stellina!" Derek calls.

"I'm coming!" I holler back, bounding down the steps.

"We can come back later and stay as long as you want," he says, plucking the key from my purse and locking the front door.

I grin. "You have no idea how many interior design conversations are in your future."

He laughs, his eyes meeting mine. "If I told you I'm happy to have them, would you believe me?"

I stare into the dark depths of his eyes and see the love shimmering there. "Yes," I say simply as my phone rings.

"You gonna get that?" he asks as we walk toward his car.

I nod and swipe to accept the call. "Hello?"

"Allegra, hey!" a warm, female voice says.

"Hi," I say slowly, wracking my brain to place the familiar tone.

She laughs. "It's Vivi!"

I grin. "Vivi! Hi! I was trying to place your voice."

"Yeah, I'm calling from the LA office."

My heart rate picks up. "You're in town? For how long?"

"Just until Monday. But I wanted to chat with you while I'm here. Tom and Jay, who interviewed you a few weeks ago, were super impressed."

My heart thuds and I falter. "Thank you."

Derek glances at me and I shake my head as my nerves ping erratically.

"Unfortunately, the position you interviewed for has already been filled."

"Oh," I manage as disappointment settles in my stomach.

"You were overqualified for it," Vivi continues.

"Sorry?" I ask. It was an entry-level position...

"Allegra," Vivi says. "I'm calling to offer you the position of regional manager."

"What?" I gasp.

Vivi chuckles. "You would be overseeing the position you originally applied for, as well as another program we're starting up. The position would entail more management and leadership qualities, which I, as well as Tom and Jay, agree you possess. I saw you dive in and do the work last summer and also spoke to your current manager about the work you've done this year in LA. Although you wouldn't be working in the field much since this role requires you to work from our head office in LA, I think you're a great fit for the position." She continues to explain the job description as I hold my breath.

Derek opens the car door for me, and I slip inside.

When he pulls away from the curb, he places a hand on my thigh in a show of solidarity. I relax under his touch.

"I know this is a lot to process and it isn't what you originally applied for—"

"It's better!" I cut Vivi off.

She laughs. "Are you interested?"

"Yes! A thousand times, yes. Thank you, Vivi. Thank you for thinking of me."

"You earned this, Allegra. You're passionate and committed and driven. I'm really sorry, by the way, about what happened. How are you doing? Feeling?" She lowers her voice.

I swipe a hand over my ribs absent-mindedly. I glance at Derek and grin. "I'm doing okay. Much better than last month."

Derek rolls his eyes.

I chuckle. "Thank you for the flowers you and Claire sent."

Vivi breathes out in relief. "I'm glad to hear it. I need to fly back to Boston on Monday night. I know it's last minute but if you can pass by the office Monday morning, I can go over the contract with you. And we can have lunch," she tacks on.

"I'd love that. I'll be there Monday morning. I can't wait to see you."

"Same!" Vivi squeals. "I'm so excited for this."

"I'm beyond thrilled," I tell her.

"See you Monday," she says.

"Thanks, Vivi." I disconnect the call.

"What's going on?" Derek asks.

"You're not going to believe this," I say.

He pulls into the Beirut parking lot and puts the car in park. Giving me his full attention, he smirks. "Try me."

I wave my phone at him. "I got a job offer!"

Genuine joy washes over his face. "The job? In LA?"

"Even better," I gush.

His smile never slips. Doubt doesn't fill his eyes. Nothing changes the pride that flares in the depths of his irises. "Tell me."

"It's a managerial position, overseeing those programs. In LA!" I exclaim.

"Fuck, baby," Derek swears, reaching for me. He grips the back of my neck and pulls me in for a hard kiss, always cognizant of my lip. "I'm so proud of you," he murmurs.

I giggle. "I'm so excited. And surprised. I, I feel giddy!" I laugh, half breathless with the excitement of the last hour.

Derek's eyes bore into mine. Smooth like whiskey, deep like forever. "You earned this, Stellina. You deserve every good thing in this life. And in the next one."

"I go in on Monday to sign. And see Vivi," I add.

Derek grins. "Congratulations, love. The Harrison Foundation is lucky to have you."

I squeal and toss my arms around him for another hug.

His hand palms the center of my back and I relax into him. This is one of the best days of my life and I want to savor it for an extra second.

"WHAT, YOU GET LOST?" Levi hollers when we enter Beirut.

Nova cheeses hard. "Nah, my girl got some action!"

Beside me, Derek blushes. He straight up blushes.

Nova and I share a look and crack up as Levi swears.

"What are you all doing here?" I ask Nova and Ivy as I pull them into hugs.

"Kenny's on her way," Ivy says.

"I'm here!" Mckenna announces, barreling her way into our huddle.

"Derek asked us to come..." Ivy trails off, glancing at my boyfriend.

I spin in his arms and grin at him. "You planned this?"

"Yeah," he admits sheepishly, ducking his head.

"But Mom really did speak to Dex's lawyer. He's been solid, helping her navigate things with Dad." Levi glances at Dex, his expression thoughtful.

"Here you go!" Devy announces, setting a tray filled with tequila shots on the nearest table. She winks at me. "Dex says welcome home. Go wild, but not too wild."

I lift a shot glass in Dex's direction. *Thank you*, I mouth.

He lifts his chin in my direction and continues to pour my mom—my mom!—a glass of wine.

"Damn. Do you think your dad"—Nova points at Derek —"has a thing for your mom?" She gestures toward Levi.

"That could get awkward," Ivy mutters.

Levi blanches while Derek laughs.

"You're a fucking troublemaker," Derek tells Nova.

She grins until her dimple appears. "It's the best part of my personality."

"Not true," Mckenna chimes in. "You're layered. Multidimensional."

"Really?" Mav remarks, batting his eyelashes at her. "How would you describe me?"

Mckenna's expression cools. "An egotistical pain in the ass."

Mav chuckles. "You're into me, babe. I knew it."

"I can't believe I stuck around for this," Mckenna jokes, rolling her eyes and tossing back a shot. She draws cheers from me, Ivy, and Nova.

"You guys! I have news!" I announce.

Levi tosses an arm around my shoulder and grins. "More than moving in with this chump?" He hooks his thumb toward Derek.

"Hey, this chump put the house in my name," I remind my brother.

He laughs and gestures for our mom and Dex to join us.

"What's going on?" Mckenna asks, when our huddle is complete.

"Well..." I wrap my other arm around Derek's waist. "Derek and I are moving in together."

"Obviously," Nova comments, twirling her finger to hurry me along.

I grin. "And I got a job offer from the Harrison Foundation!"

A collective cheer rings out.

Ivy pulls me into a hug. Levi thumps my back. Mav carefully picks me up and spins me in a circle.

"You did it!" he exclaims.

"This is real life!" I yell back.

The two of us laugh.

Jameson passes me a shot glass.

The group lifts our tequila, Levi and Dex hold cans of sparkling water, and we clink them together.

"Congratulations!" Mom exclaims, wrapping me in a hug.

I hug her back.

"I'm so proud of you," she whispers. "You did all the things a part of me always dreamed you would."

The vulnerability in her tone, the awe mixed with hope, brings tears to my eyes and I blink rapidly. "I'm glad you're here."

"Me too," she says, pulling back. Her smile is warm even as her eyes tear. "I'm so happy to witness your happiness. Your success. I missed so much, but I got to see this."

I squeeze her hand. "Are you staying for a while?"

Her eyes dart to Dex for a second before meeting mine. "Dex's lawyer is helping me sort things out, but yes, I'm going to stay as long as I can."

"Thank you, Mom." I press a quick kiss to her cheek.

"Thank you, Allegra," she whispers back.

Dex steps beside her and touches the center of her back with one hand while passing her her wine glass with the other. "Do you like the Pinot Grigio?"

"Pardon?" Mom asks, her eyebrows knitting together. She isn't much of a wine drinker.

Dex grins. Those whiskey eyes flash.

Levi groans and Derek snickers.

"I'll pour you a Riesling next. Seems we've got a lot to celebrate," Dex comments. He grins at my mom, all confidence and charisma.

"The Rousells are back," I agree. "Reunited."

"So are the Maddens," Derek says, dropping his father's name like he just claimed it.

At the emotion that crosses Dex's face, he realizes it too.

"Can we get another round of shots, Devy?" Derek calls out.

"Coming right up!" Devy promises.

Nova's eyes glimmer excitedly as she takes in the dynamics unfolding around us.

"This is intense," Ivy murmurs, her eyes darting between my mom, Dex, Derek, and me.

I laugh and nod, but I can't stop smiling. This moment, this day, is too bright. Overflowing with so many feels I want to hold on to and keep forever.

"Here ya go," Devy says, dropping off another round.

Dex passes one to Mom who looks truly scandalized.

Levi groans and I shoot him a look, wondering how he's holding up in this party environment. "You doing okay?"

His expression softens and he dips his head. Shaking his sparkling water can, he winks. "Never better, A."

"To all of you," Mom says, raising her shot in a formal toast. "May your futures be as bright as your smiles are today!"

"To the next chapter," Dex echoes.

"To the rest of our damn lives," Nova calls out.

"To the future," Ivy corrects.

"To our friendship," Mckenna says.

"To us," I add. "All of us."

I down the tequila shot and turn toward Derek. His hand is waiting, already holding a lime dipped in salt. I grin and bite into it, recalling that night from summer when we had the same exchange.

Then, the air between us tightened with tension. Anticipation.

Now, it vibrates with want. With love. With trust.

"Thank you," I murmur.

Derek swoops down and captures my lips with his. He licks the tequila and lime from my bottom lip and smacks his together. "Thank you, beauty."

"So, this is it," Ivy says, glancing around Beirut. "You're staying here, in LA, for your dream career with your dream guy."

I look up at Derek and grin. "Yeah, I guess I am."

"I want to see your house stat," Nova interjects. "And if you need help decorating..." She lifts her eyebrows.

"Or a roommate." Mav raises his hand.

Jameson scoffs.

I bite my bottom lip. "We do need to throw a house-warming party."

Beside me, Derek straightens.

"What?" I ask.

He shakes his head. "Nothing." He pulls out his phone.

"We'll have a BBQ, a fun summer bash, at our place, before you leave, Kenny. When are you heading to Boston?"

"August 22," she replies.

"Give me a date, Stellina," Derek says.

I frown.

"August 17," Nova supplies helpfully.

"Done." Derek slips his phone in his pocket.

"What's going on?" I ask.

Derek grins. "Dre said he'd come out when I have a housewarming."

I laugh. "And?"

His phone beeps. He pulls it out to glance at it. I love witnessing the grin that cuts his face. "He'll be here."

Levi wraps an arm around my shoulders. "We'll all be there. After all, we're family."

I glance around the little group of faces I love best. "Yeah," I agree. "We are."

The Clovers start talking about a band they know in Boston. Ivy and Nova pull me out to a makeshift dance floor. The lights dim, Beirut pulses to life around us, and I lose myself in the moment.

Surrounded by my best friends. With the love of my life. Joined by my mom and Levi and my found family, The Burnt Clovers, the girls, Dex.

I'm finally home.

Derek

"BUCK WOULD'VE GOTTEN a kick out of this," Dre tells me, smacking a hand on my back, as I turn chicken wings on the grill. The tangy scent of barbecue sauce scents the air and a gentle breeze whispers through the trees.

The sky is a cotton candy swirl, all purple and pink, and the temperature is starting to dip after a hot day. I pull in an inhale and let it out slowly.

Glancing at my old friend, I grin. "Yeah, he would've." I look around the yard and take in the long picnic tables adorned with fresh flowers. There's a corn hole game going on between Levi and Jameson beside the deck. Nova's laughter pierces the air as her boyfriend, West, dips down in the pool and rises with her perched on his shoulders. My dad sits poolside, chatting amicably with Mav, who's lounging in a flamingo floatie. Buck would've loved this. These people, this night, this moment. "I wish he was here."

"Me too," Dre agrees.

"I'm glad you came out, brother."

"Same. Had to see what the big deal about LA is." He smirks. "And Sarah made me promise to hand deliver her new lyrics."

I pat the pocket of my jeans where I slipped the folded-up paper Dre passed me earlier. "I can't wait to read them. She's really turning into a songwriter."

"It's her dream," he says, taking the tongs from my hand. "Let me take over for a bit. You go...mingle."

I arch an eyebrow. "Mingle?"

Dre shrugs. "Get in on that corn hole game, or pour Johan another tumbler of whiskey, or kiss your pretty girlfriend."

"I'll take you up on option C." I pat his shoulder. "Thanks, man."

"No problem," Dre says, as I turn toward Allegra.

She's sitting on the deck, relaxing with a margarita in hand. Mckenna, Ivy, and Mrs. Rousell are around her, the four of them deep in conversation, their hands moving as quickly as their mouths.

When she sees me approach, her smile widens and I wink at her. She excuses herself from the group, and moves toward me.

"How's manning the grill?" she asks, stepping into my frame. Her arms snake around my shoulders.

I grasp her waist. "I got booted off by Dre."

She looks over at Dre, in his element, and laughs. Then she glances around our backyard, drinking in our family and friends, all mingling and joking and relaxing together.

Hendrix dives into the pool and Mav cheers.

"Mckenna, you want to take a swim?" Mav taunts Kenny.

She rolls her eyes and ignores him.

"Mav's driving Mckenna nuts," Allegra admits.

I chuckle. "Now that he knows he can get to her, he's not going to quit."

"True. I'm glad Hendrix came," she comments.

"And Dre," I add.

"Yeah," Allegra says, shifting to lean into me.

I hug her closer. "Are you happy, Stellina?"

She gazes up at me, her eyes twinkling. "Happier than I ever thought I'd be."

I press a kiss to the center of her forehead. "I'm glad."

"We're lucky, Derek," she says.

"Yeah," I agree, letting the laughter of our loved ones wash over me. I tighten my hold on my girl, enjoying this simple moment that's filled with tender emotions. Nostalgia and affection. Gratitude and purpose.

And the elusive magic I've been chasing for a long-ass time.

"We fought hard for our happily-ever-after," Allegra admits quietly. "For our love."

"Stellina," I say, glancing down at her. Dipping my head, I capture her lips in mine and spill my words into her mouth. "I was never going to give up on you. On us. A love like ours..."

"What?" She pulls back slightly, her eyes searching mine.

"A love like ours doesn't quit. No matter what. Me and you, baby..."

"We're forever," she finishes my sentence.

"Forever," I confirm.

"Hey, lovebirds!" Nova calls out, waving at us. Water drips off her arms as she dances in the pool.

West holds up a football. "We're playing a game."

"In the water?" Mckenna looks skeptical.

"Loosen up, Mckenna," Mav chirps. "It'll be fun!"

"I'm in!" Ivy says, removing her cover-up and making her way toward the pool.

Dex slips into the water.

Allegra bumps her hip against mine. "What do you say?"

I snort. "I don't know a damn thing about football."

"You're all right," Allegra assures me over her shoulder as she walks toward the pool. "I can carry this for the both of us." She slips out of her cover-up and I groan at the bright red bikini she's wearing.

"Good. Because my eyes won't be on a fucking ball when they can be undressing you," I murmur, following her.

Damn, I drink in her curves. I love how self-assured she is. As Allegra saunters toward her girls, I recall the seventeen-year-old, never-been-kissed version of her I first met. There are still traces of that girl. Her sweetness. Her goodness.

But now, she's got an edge. A confidence that is so damn sexy, it renders me speechless.

The truth is, I've always been in love with my Stellina. Every single version of her. I've loved watching her evolve to become the woman she is today.

Loyal. Steadfast. Giving.

Everything I've always desired.

Mine.

Allegra

"Mama, are we going to eat French fries in Paris?" Stella asks me, her eyebrows bending toward each other. She's so serious sometimes, it's hard not to laugh.

"Stella! They don't eat French fries in France. They eat crepes!" Drake corrects her.

"They can eat fries too, Drake," Stella shoots back.

"Mom, I'm all packed," my eldest, Christian, announces, walking into the room.

"What time are we leaving?" Katelyn wonders.

"You sure you want to go on this tour?" Derek questions, his gaze darting between our four children and me. His mouth quirks into an amused smirk.

"Yes!" Stella jumps up and down on the couch, clapping her hands together. "I want to see the Fiffel Tower!"

"It's Eiffel Tower," Drake corrects her.

Stella sticks her tongue out at him. Christian taps the back of Drake's head, admonishing him.

I chuckle. "I can't wait to go on this tour," I tell Derek the truth.

"Yeah, Dad, we want to see you on stage," Christian says. At eight years old, with three younger siblings, he's a mature and thoughtful boy, enamored with his father and wanting to be just like him.

"And Uncle Levi," Drake adds.

"And Uncle Mav!" Stella shouts.

"I hope he wears those leopard pants again." Katelyn laughs.

I roll my eyes. My kids are lucky to have three amazing uncles in their lives to make them laugh with wild stories and funny antics now that Derek has to act like a parent, doling out consequences and adhering to bedtimes.

"You guys worked hard on this album," I remind Derek.

Since we married eight years ago, our life has been a whirlwind. At first, we split our time between LA and Boston, although now with the kids, we're more firmly rooted in the Golden State. Christian and Katelyn turned our worlds upside down in the best way possible. A few years later, we were blessed with the twins, Stella and Drake.

Since becoming a father, Derek took a big step back from his career, wanting to pour his time and energy into the kids, into our family, rather than lyrics. But I know he misses the Clovers. He misses songwriting. He misses the camaraderie of the band.

The past two years have seen a lot of changes for the Clovers, but their friendship, their love of music, and their bond have remained intact. And now... "It's time for a reunion."

"Yeah," Derek agrees, grinning at me. "This is going to be the best tour yet."

I chuckle as Drake shoots a Nerf dart at Katelyn, narrowly missing her face. "I don't know about that."

He looks around at our family. The suitcases are lined up by the front door. Katelyn is ignoring Drake and placing headphones in her backpack. Christian is fiddling with his new watch. Stella and Drake are now engaged in a wrestling match on the ottoman.

It's controlled chaos, a constant state of the better part of the past decade. And yet, I don't think we've ever been happier.

Or more in love. With our family, our lives, or each other.

Derek sits beside me on the couch and wraps his arm around my shoulders. I lean back into his chest as he presses a kiss to the side of my head. "I do," he murmurs. "Being on tour with all of you...music and family coming together. It's more than I ever dreamed possible."

I glance at him over my shoulder. Get lost in his deep whiskey eyes. Smile. "I hope all your dreams come true, Derek."

He smirks and gives me a peck on the lips.

"Gross," Drake sneers.

Derek and I smile.

"They already have, Stellina. You made them all come true," Derek says softly, lifting his chin toward our children.

I settle back against him, and we watch as our kids finish packing up for Derek and the Clovers international reunion tour.

First stop, Paris.

ACKNOWLEDGMENTS

All of my thanks and gratitude for the love, encouragement, and friendship that supported me as I wrote Derek and Allegra's tumultuous story.

Amy Parsons, Becca Mysoor, Erica Russikoff, Virginia Carey, Melissa Panio-Peterson, Sheila Dohmann, Dani Sanchez, Kate Farlow at Y'all. That Graphic, and Amber — thank you infinitely!

Much love and many thanks to the book bloggers, bookstagrammers, booktokkers, and book lovers for shouting out this trilogy and showering my characters with love! I appreciate you and your support!

To my home team, I love you all the world. Thank you.

The Burnt Clovers Trilogy:

Rebellious Rockstar

Resentful Rockstar

Restless Rockstar

Tennessee Thunderbolts:

Hot Shot's Mistake

Brawler's Weakness

Rookie's Regret

Playboy's Reward

Hero's Risk

Bad Boy's Downfall

Boston Hawks Hockey:

The Sweet Talker

The Risk Taker

The Faker

The Rule Maker

The Defender

The Heart Chaser

The Trailblazer

The Hustler

The Score Keeper

Standalone

Corner of Ocean and Bay

ABOUT THE AUTHOR

Gina Azzi writes Contemporary and Sports Romance with relatable, genuine characters experiencing real life, love, friendships, and challenges. Dive into her hockey romance series: Ottawa Huskies, Boston Hawks, and Tennessee Thunderbolts or get lost in her rockstar romances in The Burnt Clovers trilogy.

A Jersey girl at heart, Gina has spent her twenties traveling the world, living and working abroad, before settling down in Ontario, Canada with her husband and three children. She's a voracious reader, daydreamer, and coffee enthusiast who loves meeting new people.

Connect with her on social media or through www.ginaazzi.com.